FEAR

Other Novels by Simon Lane

Still Life With Books

Le Veilleur

FEAR

a novel

Simon Lane

Bridge Works Publishing Co.
Bridgehampton, New York

Library of Congress Cataloging-in-Publication Data

Lane, Simon, 1957–
Fear : a novel / Simon Lane. — 1st ed.
p.   cm.
ISBN 1-882593-22-7 (alk. paper)
I. Title
PR6062.A5324F43   1998
823'.914—dc21   97-42367
CIP

2   4   6   8   10   9   7   5   3   1

Book and jacket design by Eva Auchincloss

Printed in the United States of America

First Edition

For Blue

I look to the sea, to the sky, to what is
unintelligible and distantly near.

Henry Miller, *Tropic of Cancer.*

His smile tucked up his skin back
of one ear like satin skirts held high
from a rainy pavement.

Zelda Fitzgerald, *A Couple of Nuts.*

PART I

1 ❧

Dimly, dimly
The day breaks at Akashi Bay;
And in the morning mist
My heart follows a vanishing ship
As it goes behind an island.

I am staring into a blank screen. Well, blank is perhaps not the right word. The French would say *vide*, but that's not right either. *Vide*, as anyone who has run out of gas will tell you, means empty, but it also means void. Yves Klein was always talking about the *vide*, when he wasn't jumping into it. He was a good artist and he died young. He once lived in Japan. Did he also like haiku?

The screen is neither empty nor a void, but one could quite easily describe it as *vide* and get away with it. You can get away with a good deal in French. It is a language that is generous with meaning and rather less so with veracity. This has its advantages and its disadvantages, like everything else.

The computer is switched off, of course, so the blankness of the screen simply indicates its *offness*. It is otherwise very far from blank. Its lack of blankness comes from its reflection and from the bulk of hardware behind and around it. It also comes from my imagination, which allows shapes and forms to appear as if they emanated from the very depths of its being. It is a cliché to suggest that a machine has a soul, but I have nothing against clichés, even if I am a little prejudiced when it comes to computers.

Naturally, my reflection appears in the screen. Am I being vain in suggesting that some men have found me attractive? Probably. My eyes are a little too brown, a little too dark, hardly sparkling, yet oddly reflective given the right lighting and no more than two cocktails. The facial structure is strong, all in all a decent sort of profile, what is described as a full mouth, generous lips usually glossed with Cherries in the Snow, a respectfully proportioned nose, and ears no one would write home about (but then, who ever wrote home about an ear?). Nice neck, they tell me.

I found the book of haiku in my desk. The drawer is very deep, and it was only after a few days that I noticed it. It's an old book and the spine is cracked. It was opened to Fujiwari no Kintō's Akashi Bay haiku, and once I had read it I couldn't get it out of my mind.

I can see a brush hanging in space, loaded with ink. I can see the hand of the master descending, his head inclined, a wisp of hair shaking slightly as if caught in a sudden breeze. The moment is plucked from a million others before and after it; it is isolated, frozen, brought into close-up and kept there for as long as I wish, so that time evaporates, lost amid the shaft of light now seen to caress the master's brow. The master turns to me, and I feel the weight of those eyes staring right through me. I hear his voice through a thousand years of longing, metamorphosed into type so gray, paper so brown, so brittle, I fear the page might crack if I hold it too tightly. I know that what I see on the paper is only the surface, only the outward sign of something hopelessly profound. Why hopeless? Because I know I will only understand it when all has been revealed to me.

A yellowish hue emanates from the page, a lost spirit, a heart following a vanishing ship as it goes behind an island, and I am overwhelmed by it, carried off to some distant spot caught in the mist of early morning. I close my eyes for a second and allow the sunlight to form a halo of orange where the horizon was, a suitable back-drop for faraway thinking. I am in a different place now, a city filled with noise and movement and flickering light. Then I turn away.

It's time for work.

2

They made an experiment with spiders, said Fear. They injected them with different sub-stances, such as alcohol and nicotine and other drugs. And then they waited to see what kind of webs they would weave.

Fear stood at the bar, drinking a pastis and drawing on a cigarette. At the end of the counter was a young woman with a book opened up to-ward the middle and a glass of beer, partially ob-scured by an old man fiddling with some coins, transferring them from one hand to another as if somehow attempting to increase their value.

Fear stubbed out his cigarette on the floor and looked at the girl behind the bar. She was small and rather plain and had a mischievous smile. She always smiled at Fear, since the first day. It was the sort of smile that suggested she knew all about him, all there was to know. They rarely conversed — in fact, this morning was the first time he had ventured an anecdote. Usually she asked him why he was always sad.

I'm not sad.

I don't believe you.

There's not much to believe, he would answer.

Fear lived in a courtyard. The place was full of people speaking different languages — French, Spanish, Arabic, even Swedish. In the July heat, with the windows open, a continuous humming of conversations echoed around the building, dialogues of love and anger that shattered the brief periods of summer silence. He had not been there long, but he had already perceived a rhythm to the sounds and movements of those with whom he shared this corner of Paris.

His room was on the second floor of an old workshop. It didn't amount to much. A bed, a table, paint peeling from the walls and stained from innumerable leaks of water from the apartment above and from the rain that had seeped through the thick, ancient stone of the building.

Fear was penniless. He hadn't always been. But he was now. In fact, he was in debt. Even Harm had helped him out and Harm never had any money. Harm, the trickster.

So, what kind of web are you weaving? asked the girl behind the bar.

What?

What kind of web?

I don't know. I'll have to wait and see.

Wait and see?

Yes. Wait and see. That's what my mother used to call rice pudding. We used to ask her what we were getting for dessert and she would say, Wait and see. Wait and see was always rice pudding.

The girl looked at Fear quizzically and then smiled again.

It's just a story. A story you tell to a girl who smiles mischievously. Like you.

Do I smile mischievously?

Yes. That's the kind of web you weave.

You're strange. Or at least, you like to appear strange. But you're probably not strange at all. The only thing that's strange about you is that you're always sad. Even when you're telling a funny story.

That's not strange. Give me a pastis. And try to do more than wet the glass with it this time when you pour it.

The girl smiled again as she poured the pastis. And Fear smiled back at her. She knew Fear was smiling because of the game they were playing, to see how much pastis she would put in the glass, but she didn't mind. In fact, she enjoyed it. She took the bottle, inverted it, and allowed the pastis to fall from the measure into the glass. She turned the bottle to one side, allowing the measure to fill again, inverted the bottle halfway and poured in another few drops. Then she stopped, as if someone had decided to take a photograph of her.

No more?

No more, she said.

Not even for the road?

What road?

Fear took the glass from her and added water to it from a jug. He watched the pastis change color, from a dark, reflective green to a milky color he couldn't quite define. Then he drank the pastis in silence, dropped a ten-franc coin on the counter, and took his leave.

3 ⚕

Everyone moves in circles. If you are careful, and if you have time on your hands — to kill, as the saying goes — then you might trace the circular patterns of those who move within the boundaries of this place. Time and space and distance become elements to be juggled with, parts of a larger scheme only perceived with the aid of the imagination. Everyone has an imagination. It is the only thing that makes us equals. Aside from money, that is.

The pastis had lifted Fear's spirits so that, instead of thinking about the money he didn't have, he found himself dwelling on other matters, the abstractions that fill the mind as the legs move and the head soars. Everything came to him as he strode the pavement, and he felt sublimely anonymous, wrapped in a halo of his own peculiar insignificance.

It was hot. As hot as it had been for years. The newspapers talked about how long it was since it had been so hot. It must have been hot, because the French didn't usually write articles about the weather. The English wrote articles about the weather because it always took them by surprise. Fear had left England many summers earlier, but he could still picture in his mind the headlines of the newspapers complaining about the heat and the lack of water. How could a country that produced so much rain produce so little water for everyone? And how odd that he should think of England as another country when it was his own.

The heat was intense. It made him sweat. Footprints could be seen in the pavement where tarmac had recently been laid, and he stopped when he saw a lottery ticket embedded in it. He tore the ticket away from the tarmac and stared at it for a moment before putting it in his top pocket.

He walked along the street, thinking about the lottery ticket and the heat and the women he had loved, thinking about their faces and the way they had made love. He thought about the girl from America who had once painted her body with wet limestone on a beach near Brighton, about the Italian girl who had dug her nails into his back and made him bleed as he came inside her, and about the girl he had once picked up in a bar who had asked him to tie her up.

Does it hurt?

Not if you have to ask.

As he passed other people in the street, he wondered what they might be thinking, and he concluded that they were all thinking the same thing. That's all anyone thinks about, he said to himself. We are all of us victims of desire, and there is nothing we can do about it. We rarely discuss the matter, we keep it to ourselves for the most part, yet the city is alive with our monologues, all based on the same theme, filling the air above our heads.

He looked at his watch. He was late for his appointment at the bank. This made him nervous, because there had been a change in managers. The previous manager was called Pires, and he had come from Portugal. Fear had been able to win him over by speaking to him in Portuguese and alluding to the overwhelming and monochromatic melancholy of his capital city, at the same time praising the virtues of fado music, which, in fact, he loathed. The Portuguese who move to France do not always like to be reminded of their origins, but this man was different, and he took a sympathetic view of Fear's financial arrangements, never complaining when he ran up an overdraft. He even took it upon himself to loan Fear a compact disc of fado music. And Fear gave him a book in return.

You are a poet, Fear. An anachronism in a trivial world. Our finest poet of this century, Fernando Pessoa, also had financial difficulties from time to time. One often wonders whether it was for this reason that he occasionally dressed up as a woman.

Fear had managed, for a while at least, to keep a modicum of control over his finances. Various work opportunities had presented themselves.

He had even worked in Harm's bar by the river on occasion, but it was clear he couldn't go to Harm anymore, because of the money he owed him. And there was no more work elsewhere.

The new manager was called Madame Jaffré, and she spoke French with an American accent. Fear took the seat offered to him and began to explain himself by saying that he was a poet and that he didn't make any money out of his work.

How can that be? she asked in English. You must be a good poet. You seem intelligent. I can't imagine a person such as yourself spending time doing something unless you were good at it. I wouldn't do this job unless I were good at it.

But you get paid, Madame.

Yes. I get paid. But then, this is not something I necessarily want to do. You do something you want to do. You can't have everything.

Is it not possible to get paid doing something you want to do?

It is possible. But it is not contingent. What I mean is, it is not a given.

I see.

So, what do you write about?

Hard to say. Different things. People, mostly.

We have clients who are writers. And actors. Do you act?

I can act. I have done a lot of things. Too many things.

Yet writing keeps you in debt.

You could say that, yes.

I didn't say it, said Madame Jaffré. You said it.

Did I?

11

I've looked at your file. I see you made an arrangement with Monsieur Pires to pay off your overdraft in monthly installments.

Yes, that is correct.

There must be means for you to earn money. Did you know that they are casting at the moment for *The Marquis de Sade?*

No, I didn't.

One of my clients told me this morning.

The Marquis de Sade?

Perhaps that could be something for you?

I'm writing at the moment.

Well, why don't you write something commercial?

Commercial?

Yes. Commercial. An erotic novel, perhaps.

Fear looked at Madame Jaffré. And Madame Jaffré looked back at Fear, the hint of a smile creasing her lips. Meanwhile, she continued, I'll have to take your checkbook from you.

4 ❧

Everyone moves in circles. The airplane overhead is told to wait its turn. We're in a holding pattern, sorry for the delay, the pilot says, turning the stick to his right so that the city comes into view, flattened by perspective, made smaller, even intimate, by the vast horizon and open sky.

For a moment, Paris loses its attributes, it becomes otherworldly, alien, abstract, a nameless entity punctuating a greater landscape of neat fields and highways, an island amid a sea of gray and brown, but then its landmarks come to rescue it from obscurity, just as a smile, or a wince, turns a stranger into an old friend fighting his way through a crowd: the Eiffel Tower, La Défense, Montparnasse Tower and, of course, Montmartre, this last so much taller and more imposing than the pilot remembers it, even though he was here not one week before, looking out through the same cloudless window.

Somewhere to the left, or east, of center, Fear sat at his table, feeling the heat around him. He had found a pair of shorts in a drawer, left behind by the previous tenant. They were three sizes too big for him, and he had used an old tie as a belt. He sat at the table which was his, by the window, looking out onto the courtyard. In the apartment opposite he could see the composer practicing at his piano, and to his right, he heard the voices of the Arab family and a girl calling out someone's name. A woman screamed somewhere, for a reason he would never know — pain, ecstasy, a cry for attention in a world too busy to take notice.

He thought about himself, about his life, about the illusion of time stilled that so artfully aroused his senses. He never talked to anyone about his work, let alone what it was about, and it seemed odd to him that the only person who knew what he was doing was a bank manager, albeit his own. But then, all he had said, had he not, was that he mostly wrote about people?

He had lain awake the previous night, thinking about what Madame Jaffré had said and fantasizing about writing an erotic novel, wondering what sort of life his new bank manager led, what sort of world she inhabited away from the dull confines of her desk and her computer, which so shamelessly revealed the worth, or lack of worth, of those citizens under her charge. Everyone had their fantasies, everyone could become someone else if they wished, and he found himself dreaming of reversing roles with her, so that she was writing an erotic novel and he was behind her desk, dispensing kindness and austerity to those who came to visit him.

What would her erotic novel be about? A girl unable to fall in love, who could only have sex with strangers? A woman who took pleasure in imagining her lover in the arms of another woman? Making love with another woman while her lover looked on, helpless, redundant?

He had arisen at dawn, as he always did, and had sat at his table with a coffee and a cigarette, writing for the sake of writing, knowing that only the act itself would lead him forward. He remembered a book from childhood, a novel in which a man discovers a hole in the wall of his hotel bedroom and becomes a compulsive voyeur. He had started reading it and then put it away, back where it belonged on the top shelf of his father's library.

The book had made him apprehensive. He knew that it probably contained erotic passages, the forbidden fruit of adolescence, which is why he had taken it in the first place, but he felt uneasy reading what his father had also read, and it disturbed him so much that he abandoned the task. Perhaps the real reason he stopped reading the book was that he suspected there might be a hole in his bedroom wall with an adult on the other side, following his every movement. This was a thought that had plagued him ever since, no matter how much he reasoned against it.

How much of the story was concerned with what happened in the room the narrator could see through the hole in the wall? And how much of it had to do with the narrator himself? Was he the true subject of the novel, or was he just a lonely man in a Paris hotel room, unwittingly acting as the eyes and the ears of the reader? Was he really solitary, or had he found a form of companionship in his voyeurism?

Fear got up from his table, perturbed at the thought that someone might be watching him through a hole in the wall. Then he changed into an old linen suit and headed out of his room.

5 ❧

He was glad to be outside, where the heat rose to stifle him and the sounds of the neighbors ricocheted around the courtyard. He had lost the thread of what he was thinking before going to the bank and surrendering his checkbook; there was a hole in the wall somewhere, a hole in the Paris sky, and someone was looking at him, following his actions and commenting upon them.

He laughed at the thought as he stepped into Rocket Street. The girl from the bar passed him with a carton of cigarettes tucked under her arm and smiled, giving him a strange, sidelong glance.

You're not sad today.

What's there to be sad about?

The girl continued on her way up to the bar and then disappeared, out of sight. She was less plain than the day before. In fact, she looked completely different. Could it be the same girl? he wondered.

He walked down the street, through the place de la Bastille and thence toward the river, down boulevard Henri IV. When he reached the Left Bank, he made his way up to the rue des Ecoles. There he stopped to light a cigarette. Suddenly he realized he was standing outside the cinema where they played silent movies. He stared at the posters illustrating what went on inside, and he thought about Salt, the producer, who had hired him to come up with an idea earlier in the year. The summer heat made it feel a long time ago, but he remembered exactly what Salt had said to him.

Comedy. Tragedy. I don't care. But something pertinent to the nineties. I like to give people what they want. I pay a dollar a word. Try to keep it to a thousand words, more or less.

A dollar a word for something pertinent — seven dollars already, Fear would say to himself as he tried to come up with an idea that would please Salt and please the nineties and please his bank manager, who thought that Fernando Pessoa dressed up as a woman because of his financial difficulties. He'd even started to count in bed at night, but words were like sheep, and once he had earned forty or fifty of them he would be lost to his dreams, a flock of bank notes leaping over a fence.

It was January, and Paris was fixed in the orbit of its interminable, damp, and unforgiving winter, when only the coldest of days revived the spirit and cleared the mind for invention. At the time, Fear lived in an apartment not far from the cinema. He had never kept still, never stayed in the same place for more than a year, and he was upsetting the averages by keeping an apartment he had once shared and which he could no longer afford. He had left England when he was eighteen — it was as if someone had given him a push of such momentum that he would keep moving until the day he died. He never ran away from places, he just turned in circles, some increasing, some decreasing, like the world viewed from a falling star.

The poster outside the cinema was for a movie Fear had seen countless times, in which Buster Keaton plays the part of a projectionist. Toward the end of the movie, Buster ends up heartbroken. He falls asleep while projecting a film and dreams of walking up the aisle of the cinema to the stage on which the screen is set. He stands in front of the screen and imagines becoming part of the film, but the backdrop keeps on changing, so that when he tries to sit on a park bench he lands in a heap on the pavement and when he thinks he is diving into water the image of a desert flashes up behind him and he falls head first onto the ground.

When Fear handed in his thousand words,

Salt seemed initially impressed but gave him a check for only half the words earned, promising the rest on the first day of principal photography. When Fear remonstrated with him, Salt defended himself by saying that Fear had only come up with half an idea, but he relented on the telephone the next day and, in a rather patronizing tone of voice, said he would send a check for the balance and give him a bonus of ten thousand dollars when the film was made. He didn't say when that would be, he just excused himself by saying that he was walking into a meeting and that he would call him later. Salt was always walking into a meeting.

Fear moved away from the cinema and walked down the boulevard, thinking about Salt and wondering whether he would ever get the film made. Perhaps he should call him? He saw Salt occasionally. He might be sitting in a café as Fear passed by in a bus, or driving at speed down the boulevard with a look of madness in his eye, as if he were looking for someone to run over.

Fear crossed the street and dabbed his forehead. There was little shade; it was early afternoon and he saw the rest of the day stretch before him, empty of promise yet curiously inviting. He knew that all he needed to do was wait for something to come to him and that, while he did, time would stop, the sun would stay where it was, China white above his head.

The traffic moved sluggishly, retarded by the heat, and he walked, alone in a great city, his thoughts, his past, his fantasies, his whole being filling his mind and propelling him forth as if there were nowhere else to go, nothing else to do. He looked up into the heavens and the heavens looked down at him, benevolently, offering him something. And Fear took note of it, as he always did.

6 ❧

The airplane circled. Passengers to the right, then to the left, craned their necks to gain a view of Paris. Stewards and stewardesses strapped themselves in for the descent. A baby cried, and the pilot eased the stick forward, all the while looking over to Montmartre and thinking of the Pigalle Girl.

She is smoking a cigarette, he decided, a stream of blue smoke rises from her long, thin fingers as she sips her coffee and nibbles on the toasted bread made from yesterday's baguette. Or she has had breakfast already, she slips off her robe and walks naked to the bathroom, jettisoning her cigarette into the toilet and glancing at her reflection in the mirror before taking a shower. She rubs soap over her body and raises her head to the shower, closing her eyes and running her hands through her long, black hair. The soap falls and she bends down to pick it up.

Hold it there, girl. I'll get that for you.

Fear stopped and looked up. He had seen the plane fifteen minutes earlier, circling above the smog of Paris, after turning his attention from the cinema posters and walking west toward

Saint-Germain. He imagined the pilot caught in a holding pattern of desire, waiting impatiently to land so that he could once again be with the Pigalle Girl.

Fear had once spent a night with a girl from Pigalle. She had told him she was having an affair with a pilot, and every time Fear saw an airplane he thought about the two of them. He had been struck by the girl's honesty, by her lack of guile and her straightforwardness; she was hardly naive, that wasn't the point — there was something else about her that had marked him.

Everyone can be replaced, don't you think? she said to him, a smile appearing at the edge of her mouth.

The Pilot and the Pigalle Girl always seemed a good story to him, and he found himself embarking on it from the beginning as he walked the pavements and sought shade from the plane trees that lined the boulevard. It could be erotic and commercial and solve all my problems, poetic and financial, he thought. It could bring me riches and bring me closer to the Pigalle Girl, whom I liked and loved for the space of a night, never knowing her name or who she was, other than that she was honest and beautiful and most probably in love with a pilot.

Thinking of the Pigalle Girl, he did not realize that he was walking down the street on which his bank was located. He quickened his steps and crossed the street to avoid being seen. Turning a corner, however, he ran straight into Madame Jaffré. She was holding a sandwich in a bag, and she was sweating from the heat, so that moist patches appeared under her arms on the fabric of her dress.

Hello, she said, in a strangely relaxed manner, as if their meeting had been prearranged.

Hello.

I thought you should know they found someone.

They did?

Yes. For *The Marquis de Sade*. They chose an Englishman. What's his name? Boards. You're English, aren't you?

Yes.

So, they could have picked you, couldn't they? How's your writing?

It's fine.

That could mean anything.

I suppose it could, yes.

I read in a newspaper this morning that 9 percent of Frenchwomen admit to having had sex in an elevator at least once in their life.

That's nearly one in ten.

Personally, I think everyone fantasizes. I think that's how people survive. The survey also stated that 90 percent of Frenchwomen were content. It didn't say whether the 10 percent who were unhappy included any or all of the 9 percent who claim to have had sex in an elevator.

No?

I've always been amused by statistics. And surveys. I think most people lie. But then, that would be hard to prove. In a survey, I mean.

Yes, it would.

Writers make an art out of lying, don't they? We all do, in one way or another. We know we lie to ourselves, but we never accept lying in others. Such hypocrisy is one of the foundations of life and one of the paradoxes of literature.

Why paradox?

Because no matter how intelligent we might be, we are so easily taken in. That, however, has more to do with the ease with which we are prepared to lose ourselves to fantasy, the only true legacy of childhood.

You surprise me. Can it really be that simple?

Why should it be otherwise?

Because some people don't even know the difference.

Difference?

Between fact and fantasy.

And you?

Me? Make a guess.

The bank manager extended her hand, and Fear shook it, all the while thinking of the painting by Courbet with *bonjour* in the title, forgetting that the subject of the painting is two men and not a man and a woman. Then she was gone, back to her bank and her sandwich.

7 ✣

As Fear walked back to his room, the shadows grew, filling one side of the street and leaving the other exposed, blinded by sunlight. He thought about the thirty francs in his pocket, about the pilot and the Pigalle Girl, about love stories, and about his bank manager, who thought that lying was a paradox in literature. And what about

Salt? He still owes me money, he thought. Five hundred dollars. Two hundred and fifty measures of pastis.

He stopped in the bar on Rocket Street and ordered a drink from the girl who was always smiling. He looked at her carefully, at her thin cotton dress, which hung limply from her shoulders, and he tried to imagine how her body was underneath.

Pastis?

No. Chilled wine.

What sort of web will that make?

Let's wait and see.

She poured Fear a glass of burgundy and he sipped it, smarting at its acidity, all the time thinking of the girl's body and wondering whether she had ever had sex in an elevator. He could see the beads of sweat falling from her temple, and he watched her as she brushed her forehead with her arm and then turned back toward him as she bent down to fetch some milk from a cupboard, staring at her body through the dress as she moved.

She was not particularly attractive, but she became attractive as she moved this way and that, and Fear became quite hypnotized by her. She couldn't be more than twenty years old, and Fear found himself wondering whether it was her youth that attracted him to her or simply the fact that it was a while since he had seen a woman's body. I am not old, he thought. But I am still nearly twice her age.

While he drank, he thought about the woman with whom he had shared the apartment by the cinema. Her name was Gisèle, and it had lasted for almost a year, until she went to live with someone else. She already had a lover when he met her, and he thought it exciting at first that she should cheat in order to be with him. Later, she cheated on Fear and Fear cheated on her. Fear caught her one day staring at a monogrammed cufflink she had discovered beside the bed.

What do you expect? she said.

Nothing.

Exactly.

It was true that at the beginning all he had wanted was companionship and sex and he had not really loved her at all. The love came by surprise when he heard within her laughter the resonance of something eternal and when he saw, as they walked silently through the unfamiliar shade of those first weeks, an entire cumulonimbus cloud reflected in the retina of her left eye. Time might play tricks, but perspective deals a meaner hand.

Later, she was maddened by Fear's impetuousness, his eccentricity and disorder. You'll never change, Fear, she said.

People don't change. Why even mention it?

Yes, they do. They become better, if they want to. People who don't change become worse. You're worse than you used to be. And you'll get *worser*.

Fear smiled. Gisèle's English was good but there was always a moment when it let her down. He would have taken her in his arms at that point. A pattern always developed when they had an argument, a very simple pattern that tended to reduce their dialogue to a script. The words became useless in themselves, robbed of meaning by Fear's anger and frustration and by the absurdity of Gisèle's near perfect English, which she had appropriated from a BBC cassette tape. Fear tried to argue in French, because he always felt it a language better suited to the intricacies of confrontation, but she never wanted to speak her own language. Sometimes it occurred to Fear that the only reason they were together was so that she could perfect her English, a conclusion that in some bizarre way seemed to justify their mutual unhappiness.

As soon as they started having sex, though, Gisèle reverted to French. She forgot about perfecting her English and everything else that preoccupied her; she whispered to Fear in clipped phrases of love and tenderness that made him feel that they should spend the rest of their days together and perhaps record a set of tapes to teach the whole world what love was. She would sit on top of him and look upward, almost crying as she came and, when it was over, she would start talking in English again, as if signaling a return to the real world, one in which sex ceased to be abandonment and became instead an everyday occurrence, like a meal that had to be cleaned away afterward.

The girl behind the bar poured another burgundy and smiled. Did that mean he didn't have to pay for it? It tasted good as he thought about love and whether or not it could possibly die, like a person. He knew that none of the women he had loved had truly disappeared, they were still to be found somewhere in the busy passages of his heart, yet suddenly he felt devoid of sentimentality for the past; he was remembering without feeling anything, his heart was quite dormant, not busy at all, it was just his mind that was ticking, a mind fueled by the facts and incidents and accidents that made up his life; he was once again becoming a cipher for fiction, for fantasy, and all the influences that worked on an overheated brain, now cooled by the bitter wine, were nothing more than notes to be used for something, a poem that had neither beginning nor middle nor end and that always needed the artificiality of a rhyme to give it sense.

He felt numb, as if his senses had been switched off, as if the electricity had been taken out of his body and used for something else — to turn that dirty fan above his head, which only served to move the air from one spot to another and then back again in a waft of smoke and dust and burned goat cheese and something else he couldn't quite put his finger on, all turning in circles above him, making him wince and rub his eyes.

My feelings have been replaced by a form of abstraction, he thought, by the idea of what they are rather than by their own physical reality, for feelings are real, they exist, especially the bad ones, they start in the guts and seep into every corner of the body, so that when you move, people can tell what it is that moves you, they shine forth from your eyes, they lighten your step and quicken your breath.

Burgundy is the strongest wine in the world, he announced, slamming the glass onto the counter so that the stem broke off in his hand. I don't care what anyone says. It's a gut feeling. Not something you think about. If they gave it to spiders, there wouldn't be any web at all.

Then maybe you should switch back to pastis?

8 ✢

When Fear returned to his room, he sat at his table and stared through the window at the courtyard. Two of the Arab children were playing soccer, and the sound of the ball landing on the cobbles reverberated dully from one wall to the next.

Opposite, on the ground floor, the composer was at his piano. The bounce of the ball and the tapping of the piano keys created a sound of faraway beauty, a breath of childhood exhaled into the still summer air that took Fear back to a garden, a crayon tracing the path of a swallow through a sky of blank paper, and a tennis ball stuck in a hedge, fleeting glimpses of another life, gone forever yet still seen, like the wake of a ship that has long since disappeared behind an island. The ball bounced, the fingers tapped, and the metronome kept time to all that went on around it.

Fear had christened the composer Eton and his girlfriend Eve, not knowing what their real names were. They lived together on the ground floor, but Eve had a studio upstairs, where she spent most of her time. Sometimes they shouted at each other, sometimes they said nothing; it was as if whole days went by without them ever communicating. Fear often wondered how two people so different could live together. Was it true that opposite poles attracted? Who knew how it worked — it was too complex to analyze. If you could find the solution to it you would have found the key to existence.

He never greeted them in the courtyard, because he felt it might lead to conversation and an intimacy he would later regret. They didn't seem to consider him impolite; they were always deep in thought when he passed them, and they probably had no interest in him. What intrigued him, of course, was the fact that he could see them while each was unaware of what the other was doing. This gave him an omniscience that he savored. It was perhaps the real reason he didn't want to communicate with them, for, in the role of voyeur, he would have felt a hypocrite.

He had no idea what Eve did. She was a determined-looking woman in her forties with long black hair, piercing eyes, and a strong nose. She could have been Roman or Neapolitan. Eton was tall with blond hair, he was a little mysterious, he seemed to carry a secret with him, something that was not expressed in his bearing but in the way he sometimes looked out, over his piano, his hands poised above the keys, his body frozen, waiting for something to come to him. Fear was fascinated by this couple. They might both have been geniuses for all he knew, or they might equally have been lost on the periphery of their art. It didn't seem to matter. They were two people living a life that in its regularity and discipline seemed exotic to him.

He closed the window and began writing again. He described the pilot hovering over Paris, his heart beating faster as he caught a glimpse of Montmartre, the image turning in his mind of the Pigalle Girl slipping off her robe and walking naked to the bathroom, jettisoning her cigarette and stepping into the shower. She is tall and beautiful, and her legs are slender, her breasts firm, her skin smooth to the touch. The pilot imagines holding her in his arms, bending down to pick up the soap for her, rubbing her back in the shower and kissing her, his hand now caressing her breasts and slipping over her stomach to her thighs.

Fear heard a voice. The telephone was ringing, and the answering machine picked up the message.

Fear not here, I'm afraid.

It's Harm. I need the money back. I'm going on a trip. You know how it is.

Fear bent down to the floor and turned down the volume on the machine. He took the piece of paper he had been working on from the typewriter, placed it to one side, and read through what he had written. One of the keys on the typewriter was missing and he had used the dollar sign to replace it, but he decided to change this to another symbol, so he put another piece of paper into the roller and wrote once again of how the pilot imagined the Pigalle Girl as he waited to come in to land, ca*essing he* b*easts and slipping ove* he* stomach to he* thighs.

PART II

9 ❧

I keep returning to Akashi Bay. I stare at the empty screen for a while, then I open the drawer and take out the anthology of haiku.

According to the book, the master was called Fujiwari no Kintō and he lived from 966 to 1041. He is recorded as having said that *the language is magical and conveys more meanings than the words themselves express.* This is all I know about him.

Fujiwari no Kintō's haiku is a thousand years old. There is nothing about it that is pertinent to the age in which it was written, which is why it has lasted, why it is timeless. There is a ship, but there have always been ships. There is an island, and there have always been islands. There is mist and there is daybreak. And there is Akashi Bay, the place to which I have come at the beginning of the second part of a story that has yet to happen, but that will become inevitable as I discover all that is hidden, all that is left unsaid, in the haiku. I look at the book, I look at the computer screen in which my face is so enigmatically reflected, and I begin to see clues to an unfinished narrative. They come to me; all I have to do is use my intuition to make sense of them.

I imagine myself seated beside Fujiwari no Kintō. The master is frozen in an attitude of expectancy, composed and assured. I realize

I am too close. I edge away from him, trying not to break his concentration, but in so doing, I distract him even more than if I had stayed where I was. Not even this appears to ruffle him — in fact, he appears to profit from it, using the delay to consolidate what he has already made up his mind to accomplish, concentrating still further on the task ahead. There can be no room for doubt, however, for all was decided before I entered the room one hour earlier. It is still possible that a detail exists that must be resolved and integrated within the whole, but there can be no turning back now. Nothing will interfere with him.

Fujiwari no Kintō never does anything twice. If he did, he wouldn't be a master. Because I have moved, the sunlight now falls onto the floor where he has placed his writing table, kissing its feet, and the shadow of my head and shoulders no longer plays upon the rice paper. The table is very low, only an inch or so from the floor, and the master, still tall for his years, has bent his back, arching it so that his neck strains forward to achieve the most beneficial angle of approach.

I stare at the brush, hanging in space, loaded with ink. The master's hand descends, the act so clearly and so indelibly executed as to seem obvious, ineluctable, finite. A gray hair falls onto the parchment, and the master blows it clear as the first mark appears under the bristles. The bamboo shaft of the brush remains perfectly steady, meeting its shadow at an angle that remains constant to a fraction. Not a drop of ink spilled, not a line out of place, this, the perfect reduction of thought to its essence.

Honobono to. Dimly, dimly.

I can feel my heart pounding, my pulse increasing, and I feel the moisture collecting in the palms of my clenched fists, which I have now pressed into the matting beneath me. I lean forward to savor the moment when the master's brush meets the rice paper, and when it happens I gasp silently, my senses now open to the intense pleasure in seeing the haiku come to life before my eyes. The master dips his brush into the inkwell to his side and creates the second character, then the next, all in a fluid movement, with the same flourish, the same weight, the same pressure, varying the expanse of bristle from thick to thin — a broad stroke, then a narrower one, and then a broad one again — as a fresh vertical is completed, tailing off into a thin, almost transparent swath.

Akashi no ura no. The day breaks at Akashi Bay.

I look out and I rub my eyes. When I open them, I see a view as clear as crystal. The sea, foreshortened by twilight, laps over a bench of sand, its bubbling tongues appearing as if from nowhere. I move forward and step in the foam. This great swirling mass stretches from here to there, from there to eternity, uniting, dividing, leaving me stranded as if I had stepped away from the world and turned my back on it forever. I skirt the waves, ignoring the voices carried in the breeze, the desultory humming of lost love, the soft cacophony of longing, near and far, that make up its restless, salty rhythm, the damp thud of wrinkled feet marching forward, over and over again, only to retreat, like the game I still play in the back of my mind, a ghost in a corridor trying to catch me out as I turn in vain to spy him, to spy her, creeping up on me.

The master turns to me and smiles. The sea is too rough for early morning, he says. The waves do not march, how could they if there is morning mist? Imagine the sea as flat as a pane of glass, as still as a girl's face after love, when her head rests on a pillow and a smile has come and then passed from her lips.

Of course, Master, I whisper, putting the book of haiku back into the desk and turning on my computer.

10 ✂

Paris moves back and forth, it shimmers in the July heat, and all those who are framed within and without its shadow can feel its heart beating, the passage of a Métro train under a pavement grill, the weight of its traffic sinking into the asphalt of its streets, the whine of a thousand scooters carrying bags and envelopes and money and packages and photographs of girls in ball gowns for pictures in magazines to be sold in newsstands or sit proudly on the small tables people put beside armchairs. You look down from Eiffel's tower, you look up from the pavement, you look across Concorde Square past all the bodies being dumped into carts fresh from the guillotine and you sigh and inhale the air of this place. And it can smell sweet too.

The city is full of ghosts, crowded with them. They fill the vaults down below and they march along the street, over bridges, across the water, some drowning, some flying off on a whim, sliding through space, disappearing, reappearing, vanishing forever as the clouds fall, the smog and the heat and the pressure rising up, engulfing them so that they evaporate like a drop of water spilled on an unshaded terrace table. The river claims them, over and over again, this infernal channel cleaving the city in two, swirling around the island and taking all with it as it sucks its way out to sea. And only the sea will cleanse it of all the ghosts and all the blood and sweat and shit of Paris. Paris, whose darkness and light grinds the angle of vision, making you feel alive and dead at the same time. The hospital is by the cemetery, the pharmacy is beside the bar, the life raft is hooked to the bridge, so that all eventualities are catered for, for the good and the bad, the quick and the dead.

Fear scratched himself in his sleep. He had forgotten to close the window, and the light had attracted mosquitoes. They enjoy my blood, he said, half to himself. Is it the alcohol? Fear had never known a woman to be bitten by a mosquito, and he had spent summer nights in the past intrigued and infuriated by the uninterrupted sleep of his partner. When a woman is asleep, she is further from you than you can ever imagine, he thought.

He got up from the bed and closed the window. The sky was deep blue, and there were stars dotted within it. Not a soul stirred in the courtyard and he could see Eton's piano, dormant in a corner of his apartment. He turned on the light beside the bed and lay down once again. He was caught squarely in the depth of night, and he knew that time passed at its slowest here, robbed of anything to do with itself.

He lit a cigarette and looked up at a spider's web hanging from the ceiling. Why did it move about so when there was no breeze, not the slightest waft of air within the room to disturb it? He watched the web dance in the light, sending a shadow that swayed back and forth, over his legs and then away toward his desk. It was an ill-formed, inconsequential web, the work of a spider who was lazy, or drunk, or mad perhaps.

He picked up a piece of paper from the floor and looked at it for a while. It was the beginning of the love story between the pilot and the Pigalle Girl. The shadow of the web moved over it, and he watched a line of darkness sway over the typewritten words. The words came together well and he was stirred by them, by his own fantasy of the girl with whom he had once shared a night. He saw her differently now, she had become a fictional character, and he wondered how it would be if he ever saw her again. Would she be more or less desirable when she stepped forward into reality?

He glanced at his jacket hanging limply over the chair beside his desk, and he thought about the five francs remaining in the side pocket. Half a pastis. He thought about the five hundred dollars Salt still owed him and about the commercial viability of his erotic novel. How many pages should it be? What form was it supposed to take? All he knew about erotic novels was that they could only succeed if the erotic interludes were punctuated with nonerotic narrative. A certain amount of caprice, of seduction, had to take place. Mustn't forget that, he said to himself.

Then he thought about the money he owed Harm. One day Harm will come for me and, when he does, I should be ready for him.

11 ✂

The pilot had landed. He lay beside the Pigalle Girl and kissed her. She remained perfectly still as the pilot's hand moved from her left shoulder to her right breast, his index finger describing the path of a Boeing 747 on a routine flight from Paris to Los Angeles.

The plane headed northward when in fact it could only have been west, away from the sun, seeking out her right nipple and landing on its outer edge. He circled carefully, dabbing his finger with moisture from his tongue so that a trail of saliva marked its passage, and then he lowered his mouth to it and touched it with the tip of his tongue. As he did so, he continued the flight of his other finger, creating a line from her breast to her thighs, drawn in rhythm to the movement of his tongue, which approximated to the angle of descent into Los Angeles airport. When his hand reached her pubis, the finger turned in circles around it, caught for a moment in a holding pattern that allowed the pilot to strain the Pigalle Girl's entire body. Her body arched upward from the bed, and her hips moved from side to side in an attempt to coax the errant finger inward to the very core of her being, to that miniscule lump of tissue now wet, erect.

The pilot continued circling, turning his finger, turning his tongue, and when he finally moved to the Pigalle Girl's clitoris she cried out sharply, sinking her fingers into his hair and scratching his scalp so that he turned away in pain. His head moved down her body, his hands grasped her breasts, he slipped one leg over hers and slid his tongue from her navel to her neck and then back down again, placing his lips on her vulva. She tasted salty, and when she came he heard the murmur of the sea, a tongue of water drawing back within itself, scouring the beach as it disappeared forever, back from whence it had come, lost amid a thousand others, all turning and falling without end. Then he pushed himself inside her, taking her body in his arms and lifting her from the bed as he moved slowly back and forth. He kissed her neck, he kissed her ear, and when he came she came again with him, never saying a word, just breathing deeply, sweetly against his chest.

I missed you, she said.

40   I missed you too.

I miss you now. Do what you just did. Let's see if the same thing happens.

How about a martini first?

Martini afterward.

Where do you want to go?

Los Angeles.

We've just been to Los Angeles.

Let's go there again.

I'm tired of Los Angeles.

I'm not.

OK. Los Angeles. But first, a martini. No Los Angeles without a martini. Is it a deal?

It's a deal. But no cheating this time. Remember, it's nine thousand kilometers. And that takes more than fifteen minutes.

I circled, didn't I?

Yes, you circled.

I kept my holding pattern.

Yes, you kept your holding pattern.

So, all things considered, it's time to get the shaker out.

12 ❧

Fear swore. He had turned off the ringer on the telephone, and he had turned down the volume on the answering machine, and he had wrapped the answering machine in a sweater, and he had put the answering machine and the sweater into his suitcase and jammed it shut, cutting a hole in the lip of the case with his Swiss army knife so that the lead would be able to pass through. But he could still hear a distant click when someone

called, followed by his own voice, muffled, un-
real, echoing within the case as if he, and not just
the tape, were lodged inside. Nevertheless he felt
constrained to kneel on the floor and put his ear
to the suitcase to hear who it was.

Perhaps we could meet, said the voice.

He didn't recognize who it was at first. He
heard a name but he couldn't decipher it. Angry and frustrated at allowing himself to be in-
terrupted, he nevertheless felt comforted by the
voice; it sounded gentle yet authoritative. He
opened up the case and played back the tape. It
was Madame Jaffré.

I trust all is well. We should meet again soon
to discuss matters.

Fear went back to his desk and reread what he
had written, and then he had the pilot and the
Pigalle Girl make love again. *The Pigalle Girl's
head swayed from side to side, sweat appeared
on her chest and on her temple, she closed her
eyes then opened them again and lashed out with
her arms, knocking the martini shaker from the
bedside table to the floor as the pilot lost himself
within her sleek young body.*

He looked out through the window. The soccer ball appeared from the other end of the courtyard and struck the wall beside Eton's piano
room. The hollow crack it created resounded in
time to the pilot as he came inside the Pigalle
Girl, and he smiled as he finished the chapter,
pulling the paper from the roller of the typewriter and laying it carefully to one side.

Everything is timing, he said to himself, lighting up a cigarette. Or practically everything.

He reread the chapter in its entirety and wondered whether the erotic sections were up to the mark. He liked the pilot and the Pigalle Girl; he thought they were good characters. The pilot had yet to be developed, but Fear had already decided he was something of a veteran, an ex–Navy fighter pilot who had served in Vietnam — yes, he was old enough to have caught the tail end of the war, putting him in his midforties. Fear didn't want him to be any older, but he did want him to be a veteran, so Vietnam was perfect. He had to be something of a hero, courageous and scarred by experience. He had to have stared death in the face. Otherwise, it wasn't going to work.

Of course, what Fear was saying to himself was that the pilot had to be everything that he himself was not. Men and women are often attracted to the same type of person, it was true, yet they could just as easily choose the exact opposite of their former lover. Fear had done that in the past, and he could imagine the Pigalle Girl doing the same thing. Perhaps this was why she had, in real life, chosen Fear for the night, to break away from the pilot's oppressive worldliness?

The Pigalle Girl had many attributes. She was honest and direct, yet there was a palpable air of fantasy about her. She yearned for escape, she yearned to disappear. Fear was not convinced that he should use the real Pigalle Girl for the story, but he did know that nothing about her would be different physically. She was the perfect model for an erotic novel. She had a sensuality about her that was breathtaking. In terms of character, he might well make some changes as the story developed. But that could wait.

The Pilot and the Pigalle Girl was a love story that had already started, and he liked the fact that the pilot went directly from his holding pattern in the air to the Pigalle Girl's bed. Anyone buying the book in the hope that it was erotic would not have to look too far for proof. Chapter two would put them immediately in the picture. Agents and editors would also get the idea fairly quickly. The last thing he wanted was for them to think it was the story of an airplane accident. Although those sold well too, didn't they?

He turned away from his desk and called Madame Jaffré. It was essential that he handle her correctly. He had no means whatsoever to pay off his overdraft, so her role in the execution of the erotic novel was crucial. She was in a position to give him the only thing he really needed. Time.

13 ❧

Across the courtyard, Fear could see Eve working in her studio. Eton was absent for the moment. Normally he remained at his piano or at his desk beside it, working. The piano lid was up, but its keys looked as if they had never moved, as if they were stuck where they were forever. There is nothing as silent as a piano unplayed, Fear thought.

The soccer ball appeared from the other end of the courtyard and was kicked back by one of the Arab boys. A siren sounded from Rocket Street, a woman cried out as if she had been struck, and the ball came back again, missing Eton's window by an inch and bouncing back toward Fear's door below. Above Eve's studio, the man who was always carrying a six-pack of beer back from the store sat on the windowsill, looking inward to his apartment. And the ball was picked up by the Arab boy and carried off, out of sight.

Through the open window, a breeze came up from the cobbles and pushed the fresh piece of paper he had put into the typewriter from side to side, like the first leaf of autumn. As it did so, Eton appeared from the street and let himself in to his piano room, while, above him, Eve worked on at her desk, oblivious to what went on outside or below.

Madame Jaffré had asked to meet him in a café, which had at first surprised him. But as he thought about it, he realized that while he might be in a perilous situation so far as his bank account was concerned, she too was threatened. What was to stop him from simply disappearing and never paying back his overdraft? Madame Jaffré had had an air of superiority on the two times he had met her, but it now occurred to him that she might have understood the sort of person he was, that he was a problem to her as much as she was to him. While he needed to win her over in order to buy time, she needed assurance that he would pay off his debt.

He had only now started to think about the matter carefully, after hearing her voice on the answering machine and learning that she wished to meet him again. The voice itself had changed slightly. Had she had second thoughts about him? Had she had a meeting with a superior? What was going on, exactly?

Madame Jaffré had suggested that Fear come to the bank first and that they then go to the Armistice around the corner, off place Saint-Sulpice. Fear knew the Armistice well. And the waiters knew Fear. He would rather have gone somewhere else, as he had a tab there, but he couldn't tell Madame Jaffré that. He decided to suggest a change when he met her in the bank, and he would think of some reason to justify it.

He didn't have enough coins for a Métro ticket, so he walked to Saint-Germain. It was as hot, if not hotter, than the day before, and he loosened his tie and removed his jacket as he made his way down Rocket Street. He thought about delaying the Pigalle Girl's orgasm as he walked, then delaying the pilot's orgasm, then giving the Pigalle Girl another orgasm, and then giving neither of them an orgasm, just leaving them suspended in search of their shared orgasm as the chapter ended. Then he turned the Pigalle Girl over very gently and had the pilot slip over her back and enter her from behind. They came together just opposite the hardware store.

At the bottom of the street he switched to the other sidewalk, as he owed the Arab shop 190 francs, but the proprietor saw him and called out his name. Fear strode faster, turning back to the

man and calling out a hurried greeting to him before disappearing around the corner, only to run
straight into Agostini, the fashion photographer,
to whom he owed a thousand.

Hello, Agostini. Got to run.

How are you, Fear?

Me? Great. How about you?

I'm tired of fashion.

How can you be tired of fashion? I don't
understand it. All that money, Agostini! Just for
taking someone's picture! It's not worth thinking
about!

It's easy for you, Fear. You do something
interesting.

Interesting? What's interesting about it? I'm
trying to describe something. That's technical,
not interesting.

Technical? That's interesting. What is it?

I can't say, Agostini. I never talk about what
I'm doing. Even when I'm not doing anything.

It's a book, then. So, what's it about?

People, mostly. Look, I've got to run. You
know how it is. And don't stop taking pictures.
Otherwise we'll all end up on the street.

Fear carried on, crossing the street again and
losing himself in the crowd in front of the Café de
la Bastille before pressing on toward the river. He
smiled, almost laughing aloud. Agostini earned
more in a day than he could earn in a year. Now
that was interesting.

14 ❧

Fear reached the bank fifteen minutes late for his appointment. He had already decided not to apologize. Gisèle had constantly reproached him for his apologies, and he had given them up as a matter of principle.

The English always say sorry, came her voice, back to him. But they never mean it.

Madame Jaffré was seated at her desk, writing a letter with a fountain pen. She rose and shook his hand, smiling warmly at him. Fear smiled back and felt her hand slip from his. He now realized that he had never before seen anyone who looked less like a bank manager. As she moved around her desk, he saw that she was wearing silk stockings with thick brown lines up the back. The atmosphere was rather tense between them, and the awkwardness of the encounter was symbolized by the expression on Fear's face, which registered mute astonishment, and by Madame Jaffré's clumsy attempts to screw the top of the fountain pen back onto the barrel.

You write by hand, Madame? You don't use the computer?

I use both. And you?

Pencil. Or typewriter.

Pencil? So as to facilitate editing?

So as to save money.

Shall we go?

Yes. About the Armistice . . .

You don't like it?

It's not that. It's just that it's a little expensive. I feel embarrassed mentioning it.

But I am inevitably cognizant of the strain on your finances. I am your bank manager. So you don't have to feel embarrassed. That's very English of you.

Yes, quite.

Besides, I invited you.

They stepped out of the bank and walked down to the boulevard Saint-Germain, crossing it at the entrance to the rue de Buci. They took a terrace table at the Armistice, and Fear sat nervously on his chair. He remembered the scam he had played on one of the waiters. The waiter was a gambler. He had asked Fear whether he would put some money on a horse in the Derby for him, because there was nowhere to place a bet in Paris. Fear bought an English newspaper and found out that the horse was a clear outsider. The day before the race, he took 100 francs from the waiter and said he would place it for him through a friend in London. But he didn't have a friend in London, and he spent the 100 francs in the bar at the top of Rocket Street. The horse won at eight to one, so that was 800 francs plus the original 100-franc stake, on top of the 350 he still owed the Armistice for the champagne he had bought on the night he met the Pigalle Girl.

It's a little hot here, Fear said.

But we're in the shade.

A bead of sweat fell from Fear's temple and landed on his trousers, like a tear. He looked into the café through the window and saw two of the waiters who were serving. Then he relaxed. The waiter to whom he owed the money must be having his day off, so he was in the clear. To confirm matters, another waiter appeared to take their order. Madame Jaffré ordered an express and Fear followed suit.

How's your writing, Mr. Fear?

Fear. You can call me Fear. That's what everyone else calls me. My writing? Quite good.

Have you any means of earning money at the moment? Apart from writing, that is? You did say you could act. That you had done a lot of things.

It's a little difficult at this time of year. People seem to be packing up to go on holiday. You know how it is. But I'm working on something that might save the situation.

A book?

Well, could be a book. Yes.

The waiter brought their coffees, and Fear found himself wondering why he hadn't ordered a pastis. It was the same price.

Perhaps you would have preferred something stronger? continued Madame Jaffré, watching Fear spill coffee into his saucer as he stirred his cup.

No. I'm fine. Really. Just fine.

That's good. Although it is getting on for cocktail hour. Did you know that more peanuts are consumed per annum in the bar of the Hotel Lutetia than in Vincennes Zoo?

Fear smiled. And then he laughed.

You have an infectious laugh, Fear.

50   It's a good joke.

It's not a joke. It's a statistic. That's why it's funny.

I've never met a bank manager with a sense of humor before.

Well, I've never met a writer before who wrote with a pencil because he thought it was cheaper.

Maybe I will have that drink after all.

15 ✕

The Pigalle Girl liked to play games with the pilot. They were supposed to be going out for lunch. The pilot confessed to an interest in art and had suggested they take a taxi down to the Louvre and then have lunch at the restaurant whose name he forgot that looked out over the glass pyramid.

We should probably try to do something, he said. I spend all my time inside. Inside a plane looking at the sky, inside a room looking at the walls.

He had dressed, put on some jeans, some cowboy boots, and a T-shirt, and was standing by the window in the Pigalle Girl's apartment. The Pigalle Girl was putting on some lipstick and looking into the mirror that hung over a dresser beside the bed. She could see the pilot with his back toward her, and she smiled. She didn't want to go out. She walked over to him and turned him toward her. She drew him over to the bed and sat down on it. Then she unbuckled his belt and very slowly undid the buttons of his fly. She wanted to make love to him as she knew that he wanted her. He insisted on giving her money so she didn't have to work in the topless bar, and the only way she felt she could pay him back was by sucking him off before they went to the Louvre and the restaurant he liked. He had told her that he didn't want her to work in the topless bar because that was what hookers did, but now she felt more of a hooker than she had before, because he was paying for her and the only way she felt she could repay him was by having sex with him, whereas when she worked in the topless bar she didn't have to have sex with anyone if she didn't want to. She just had to serve drinks and smile and, by so doing, earn her keep and be able to buy things for herself and take the pilot out to lunch if she wanted.

She knew she was not supposed to think in that way, but she couldn't help feeling trapped. She knew the pilot would not allow her to go back to the topless bar and that if she mentioned that she wanted to, he would think there was something wrong with her, that she actually enjoyed men flirting with her and that she was probably a hooker at heart after all. Why should she when he had money to take care of her? he would ask.

The Pigalle Girl was an autodidact: she had read voraciously and taught herself English, and she knew about art and many other things, for that matter. But she had learned early on that the only way she was going to survive was by working in the topless bar. If she didn't do that, she would be condemned to an office desk as a sec-

retary or to the checkout counter of a supermarket, flashing bar codes over a laser box, lulled to distraction by numbers repeated and voices reprimanding her for dreaminess. The bar might be hard work, but at least she lost less time to someone else and earned enough to give herself the impression of freedom.

The pilot looked down at her as she took his prick in her hand. I want to see some art, he said. You know. Art. We don't have much art in America. We just have shops.

How is it possible that the pilot of a Boeing 747 from Los Angeles who once shot rockets from a fighter would rather go to the Louvre than be sucked off by me? she asked, taking his prick and putting it carefully between her lips so that tiny smears of purple lipstick appeared on its tip.

Anything's possible, girl. I don't expect they'll take the paintings down between now and when we get there.

The pilot's prick was not hard, but it soon became hard, despite the pilot's apparent reticence and despite his stated wish to go to the Louvre as soon as possible. He looked down at the Pigalle Girl and stroked her hair with his hands, and the Pigalle Girl sucked on his prick, moving the skin back and forth with her hand while she did so. He had never come inside her mouth and he wasn't sure whether she felt comfortable about it, but before he had time to think carefully about it he was coming and she was swallowing him. They were quite still, the pilot looking down at the Pigalle Girl and *the Pigalle Girl sitting on the bed looking up at him.*

You didn't have to do that, girl.

I wanted to.

I'm glad.

So am I.

Shall we go?

Where?

To the Louvre.

That's not very far.

Afterward we can go somewhere further. If you like.

16 ❧

Fear had only one piece of paper left. All the paper on his table had been turned over and used again, and in some cases he could no longer tell which were the good passages and which were the bad ones. Some of the ones that were good originally were less good on rereading, and some of the ones that he had earlier rejected had elements that were not improved and sometimes worsened on rewriting.

For example, he had written several versions of the previous chapter, concerned lest he give the wrong impression of the Pigalle Girl. He didn't want people to think that simply because she had worked in a topless bar she was a stereotype. The real Pigalle Girl had worked in a topless bar but was the least likely person to have done so. Had he explained that correctly? Did it really matter? How important was it to stress the fact that she was different from any other girl, in a topless bar or anywhere else — that she could not be, nor ever would be, defined by what she did, only by what she was? Or should he just forget about the topless bar altogether and not even mention what she used to do for a living? No. That would change the relationship between her and the pilot, and he needed this tension between them to justify what was going to happen, even though he had an incomplete idea of what that would be exactly.

She had to have worked in the topless bar to make the pilot jealous and want her all to himself, even though that would stifle her, making her yearn for a different kind of freedom. She had to feel trapped, gripped by the pilot's infatuation, almost suffocated. For this was going to be the last time they were together. That was the love story.

Fear put all the sheets together and read them over again, but he became disoriented while turning the page, the recto and the verso competing for attention in the same way that the courtyard competed for his attention when he was writing. The missing letter on his typewriter further confused him, for by using the asterisk he had the sensation of reading a work that had been arbitrarily censored by some unseen editor: *Smea*s of pu*ple lipstick appea*ed on its tip.*

Perhaps he should switch to another symbol? Perhaps the dollar sign would be better after all? He recalled a novel written by a man called Perec, who had used every letter in the alphabet

55

to tell his story except *e*. Had Perec had problems with his typewriter as well?

He looked at the last remaining sheet of paper and he wondered whether he should save it, start another chapter, or rewrite the previous passage. Should he continue, regardless, and then work backward through his mistakes, through all he had done, and start again at the beginning — assuming, that is, he could find some more paper?

He placed the last sheet of paper in the roller of his typewriter and stared at it, wondering at its clean, virginal beauty, and he didn't dare soil it with so much as a letter as he thought about the Pigalle Girl and about her destiny in the world of Paris and elsewhere. Men would always try to change her, try to mold her, but they would never succeed, they would all eventually slip out of her orbit with nothing but the memory of a kiss, a shared view of a street corner, a heart trailing in the wake of a vanishing taxicab.

The pilot was doomed. He was tragedy incarnate. He wanted to free her and keep her, and in so doing, he took everything away from her. He was a man of power, a veteran of life and death who was capable of understanding need, yet he was hampered by the bulk of his own ego, which had shrunk and inflated through years of insecurity and bravado, for, of course, the two go hand in hand even when they are not speaking to one another. If he learned to think of the Pigalle Girl as more than just an object of his desire, then he might be saved. Is that why, perhaps, he wanted to go to the Louvre without having sex first, to prove that he appreciated her in her entirety and that he could enjoy her ideas as much as her body?

17 ⋈

Fear got up from his table. Now there was no more paper left at all. He lit a cigarette, put on his jacket, and walked out into the courtyard and the street. He turned left, up to the café.

Pastis? Or burgundy? Tidy web? Or untidy web?

Pastis web. But you'll have to put it on the slate.

For ten francs?

Well, there's the glass I broke too.

Forget about the glass. Is that what they do in England?

What?

Make customers pay for broken glasses?

I can't remember. I think it depends on whether or not it's an accident.

Fear smiled at the girl. She was plain, it was true, but her smile resolved everything, making of her an angel as she placed a glass on the counter and inverted the pastis bottle, tipping it slightly and then holding it back the way she had done before to tease him. There was something faintly erotic about it — or was he becoming obsessive? One of these days he would have to make love to a woman, just so that he could stop thinking about sex.

Madame Jaffré had known Fear wanted a drink and not a coffee; she knew he was just being polite. It occurred to Fear that while he knew nothing whatsoever about these two women, they seemed capable of looking right through him. Especially Madame Jaffré.

Madame Jaffré was playing games with him, she had something up her sleeve. When she had asked him what plans he had for work, he hadn't dared tell her that he was writing an erotic novel, even though, if her original suggestion had been a serious one, he might have been able to offer it as a commercial suggestion, even collateral to get his checkbook back. But how could he tell whether she was serious or not?

You're less sad today, said the girl from behind the bar. More sad than when I last saw you. But less sad than the time before.

What's there to be sad about when a girl with smiling eyes buys you a pastis? Even if she does play tricks with the measure?

He looked at the girl and he thought about her body underneath her dress and he thought about Madame Jaffré's legs and about the Italian girl who had once dug her nails into his back as he came inside her and about Gisèle's habit of walking naked around the apartment and about the fact that he had no paper left and four, no, three, cigarettes left. Then he drank his pastis and, with a wave, headed out of the café.

18 ❧

Fear called his street Rocket Street because it seemed to burn up in the summer. Every time he stepped into it he saw something that startled him, making him blink or wince. Half of it had been torn down by developers, left like the aftermath of some battle or other, and it seemed to Fear that it was the destruction around him that had altered people's behavior, that, in different circumstances, this communal neurosis would lift like a fog on a February morning and all would be well, everyone would suddenly find themselves at peace with the world. But there was no peace to be had here, there were always fights, arguments, confrontations, the *clochards* screaming out for a couple of francs from some hapless commuter or local, losing their temper, cursing the demolition ball that hung over their head, recoiling from the tension so exacerbated by the July heat.

As he stepped forward, he saw the old woman with the hunched back heading down an alley with a saucepan filled with cat food, another woman lying in the doorway of a derelict shop, her hand held out to passersby, her mouth trying to find the words to an old music hall song long since banished from her mind, and three teenagers racing out of the supermarket clutching a box and laughing as a security man chased them around a corner. This was Paris, but this was Rocket Street, a tangent that led from the place de la Bastille to the place Voltaire, thence up to Père Lachaise, and anything that could happen would happen within its desultory, chipped, and piss-stained walls.

Fear followed the rhythm that set his street apart from all the others, and he stopped for a moment to take it all in, as if it were the beginning of a book that might or might not be a love story, the book he would write later on when he was living somewhere else, having earned his keep from his erotic novel, or possibly much later, when, old and tired and gray, he would write of his life for no other reason than to test his memory.

He would look up again toward place de la Bastille and then he would look left, up to Père Lachaise, the street sloping upward slightly to a lump of green, the huge trees jutting out from between the gravestones and the mausolea, the haze of sweat and mist and grief that hung like a cloud over its dull granite portals, welcoming death with open arms even as it strode along the pavement. No, it wasn't the demolition ball that drove them all crazy, it was death making its way up the hill, its face a mask, its mouth torn by a toothless grin as it bent down to salvage the stub of a cigarette from the thick, unyielding cobbles.

Fear!

It was Agostini again. Hello, Agostini. What are you doing?

I'm taking the day off. Walking around. Want to come to the movies?

Can't do it. Haven't got the time.

What happened to that movie you were working on?

The Buster Keaton story. That was a joke, Agostini.

Really? I'd like to see it.

Agostini, you know I owe you a thousand.

A thousand? I'd forgotten about it.

You've forgotten about it? Well, I'm glad I reminded you.

Don't worry, Fear. You can pay me back later.

Well, I've run out of paper.

That's not good. I mean, for a writer to run out of paper. It's like me running out of models.

Exactly.

So you need some paper. I think I've got some somewhere. What kind of paper? I mean, does it have to be a special kind of paper?

Just white. Without anything on it.

For your book?

How did you know I was writing a book?

I didn't. I just guessed. So, what's it about?

I don't know yet. I'm not sure it's about anything. It's just a story.

You'd rather wait. And not tell anyone until it's finished. Right?

When it's finished I won't have to tell anyone about it. They'll be able to read it.

When I take a picture I never know what it's going to look like.

That must be strange.

It is. Taking pictures is a mystery. But it's not interesting.

I don't understand, Agostini. Squashing the world into a neat rectangle can hardly be a dull affair.

Look, here's some money, Fear. You've got to have paper. I mean, what could be more ridiculous than a writer without paper?

PART III

19 ☡

The master turns to me. A smile spreads across his features. The language is magical, he says. It conveys more meanings than the words themselves express.

What are those meanings, Master? I ask.

That is for you to discover. My task is to create meanings. Your task is to interpret them. Now, leave me for a while. Win and Wip will take care of you.

Win and Wip are the twin geishas who came to my room last night. Win reminds me of someone for some reason, while Wip seems new and different — a paradox, obviously, as they are identical in every detail.

I was taking a bath at the time. There was a knock on my door and I got out of my bath to answer it. I asked who it was but all I could hear was giggling.

The master sent us, they said in unison. To relax you after your journey.

I let them in. They made it clear I should continue my bath, soaping my back and massaging my tired limbs. Win got into the bath with me while Wip rubbed my shoulders and washed my hair. We spent an agreeable evening together, especially after my bath, when they took turns making love to me.

I had never made love to another woman before, and at first I was intimidated, as much by the fact that there were two of them as anything else. Wip produced a dildo in the form of a bird, its wings tucked in smoothly along its back, and while Win circled my breasts with her fingers and bent down to kiss my nipples, Wip rubbed the bird's head against my clitoris. It was only then that I remembered whose precursor Win might have been, a Japanese girl in high school who once tried to make a pass at me in the back of a Volkswagen minibus.

The master needs to be alone for long periods to meditate and compose himself, but he nevertheless allows me to watch him at work. He is generous, as always, neither complaining nor making me feel ill at ease when I strike an incorrect attitude or perhaps move my weight from one knee to the other after remaining still for as long as I can. He treats me differently from the geishas because I am a Westerner and because I have traveled many miles to see him. Yet it is inevitable that he asks for some time to himself after performing his haiku, for there can be no doubt, now that I have seen it firsthand, that the writing of a haiku is a performance as much as a conceptual act, a moment of veracity in which the invisible and the visible unite to become one.

Returning to my room, I dwell on the hidden meanings of the haiku, of Akashi Bay, of the vanishing ship and the unspecified heart that watches it disappear behind the island. They are mysteries more than meanings, and I resolve one day to solve them.

Win and Wip are waiting for me. They undress me slowly, carefully folding my kimono and bathing me after the rigors of the morning. Tea is brought, and the endless ceremony for which Japan is famous stretches through the afternoon. I sit with the geishas, being served and offering observations on their country and their culture. They remain silent, occasionally giggling at my comments. They don't understand a word I am saying.

20 ✒

Fear awoke from a siesta. After taking his leave of Agostini he had gone to the stationer's and bought a ream of paper and then to the supermarket to buy a bottle of pastis. He had gone back to the bar and bought the girl with smiling eyes a drink and had stayed there for an hour, drinking at the counter and making jokes with her. Then he had returned to his room and fallen asleep.

He dreamed that he was flying through gaps in the clouds and looking down at the buildings and monuments that make up the city, turning and spinning through the air — that he was a giant standing on the banks of the Seine, lassoing the Bastille column and tearing it out of the ground so that all of Paris was sucked into the hole it created. Not even the women and children were spared, all falling into the lake below, crying and screaming for mercy as others, the ghosts of history and of the future, looked on, helpless.

He awoke, content. He knew that the release he felt at being rescued from a bad dream was infinitely more pleasurable than being torn away from a good one. The sense of loss at being unable to recapture that world that had been so artfully created for him was the loss of the ages, a lament for life itself, and he recoiled from it in disproportionate horror. Yet a dream was nothing more than the loss of proportion, a neat band of blue lining the upper edge of the sky, a head looming over an empty monument, a line bisecting a face in a permanent, wistful smile. So it was that while good dreams tended to make him sad, nightmares actually invigorated him, even while making him shake to the depths of his soul.

He went over to his table and sat down. There were 500 sheets of paper piled on one side and the change from 500 francs on the other, his defective typewriter in the middle, silent in the thick, summer air. He stared through the window and saw Eton enter the courtyard, and he watched as Eton took his key from his trouser pocket and opened the front door, closing it gently behind him. Because of the large windows on the ground floor, Fear could follow Eton's movements as he went to a cupboard and poured himself a drink before going over to his piano and resting his glass on a small round table at his side.

Soon enough, he was playing discordant music, repeating the same note over and over again and recording what he did on a sheet on the music stand. Eve worked above, deaf to Eton's work and to the other sounds that echoed in the courtyard and upward.

What did she do? wondered Fear.

He looked over to Eton again before taking

the first piece of paper from the pile and placing it carefully in the roller of his typewriter. We're all wrestling with our reflections, he said to himself, before losing himself in the miniature, elusive world of the pilot and the Pigalle Girl.

21

The restaurant was crowded, but a table became vacant as they stood on the terrace. The Pigalle Girl caught the waiter's eye and soon they were seated, looking across the courtyard of the Louvre. A man dressed as a mountaineer was cleaning the glass pyramid, and the pilot stared at him as the Pigalle Girl looked at the menu, trying to decide what to have.

Take whatever you like, girl, the pilot said, placing his hand on the table and touching the ends of her fingers.

I'll have a salad. A Niçoise.

I don't understand the pyramid, the pilot said. Is it just an entrance?

It's a pyramid. It's not just an entrance.

The waiter came and they ordered. The pilot asked for a martini and the waiter brought a vermouth with a small piece of ice floating in it, so the pilot went off with the waiter to talk to the barman. The pilot didn't speak French, and the Pigalle Girl offered to explain what he wanted to the barman, but the pilot didn't think that would work, as it would take longer for him to explain to the Pigalle Girl what a martini was and for her then to explain it to the barman than it would for him to supervise the operation, even though he didn't speak French.

But you forget, I used to work in a bar.

They didn't know what a martini was there, either.

Yes, they did. Patrick knew about martinis.

Who's Patrick?

You know Patrick. He's the barman. He comes from California, like you.

Well, we're not in the bar now.

You don't remember? When we met? You liked Patrick. That's why you kept on coming back. Because Patrick mixed a good martini.

I came back because of you.

That's not true. If Patrick hadn't been there we wouldn't have met at all, because you only talked to me after you had been to the bar a few times and after you had moved from a bar stool to the table I was attending. So we should thank Patrick, for without him, we wouldn't be here together.

Thank you, Patrick.

The pilot got up from the table and went to talk to the barman, and the Pigalle Girl looked at the pyramid and the mountaineer climbing from one pane of glass to the next, cleaning it. He should be cleaning a mountain, not a pyramid, she thought.

Now that's a martini, the pilot said, returning to the table.

Patrick would have made a better one.

I don't want to hear about Patrick.

You're jealous. Of a barman.

No, I'm not.

Yes, you are. You don't want to hear about the bar or about Patrick, even though without either you would never have met me.

But that's the past now.

Yes, it is the past. But the past is always with us. We carry it wherever we go. It can be a burden, it can be as light as a feather, but it never goes away.

I'm not interested in the past.

It doesn't matter whether you are interested in it or not. My past is important to me. One day, I will go back to it and work in the bar.

No, you won't.

Why? Are you going to take me away?

I'm not going to take you away. I want you here, in Paris.

But not in the bar.

Not in the bar.

You don't want to take me away, because you have a wife in Los Angeles and you have your children and your friends and your golf.

The pilot laughed. Golf? I don't remember mentioning golf. I don't even play golf.

All Americans play golf. They are more interested in golf than they are in anything else. An American who is good at golf has achieved a degree of perfection only rivaled by a glass pyramid.

You are angry.

I don't want to be kept like a painting in the Louvre you can look at when you come to Paris.

Who have you been talking to, girl? Have you met someone else? Why should you want

*to work in the bar when you can be free, doing
what you like?*

But I like working in the bar.

No, you don't.

*I do. But you are jealous. Even though you
have a wife. Perhaps I shall take a lover too. In
fact, I already have. I have many lovers. Men and
women.*

And women? Any golfers among them?

One or two.

How is your salad?

How is your martini?

*The martini is perfect because I mixed it my-
self. And you are perfect too. You are like a painting, and it is true that I want to keep you as such.
That's what happens when a pilot meets a girl
from Pigalle, or a girl from Pigalle meets a pilot,
whichever way you want to look at it. And after lunch we'll skip the Louvre and we will walk
across the river on the bridge that doesn't have
any cars on it and we will hold hands like two
people who have neither a past nor a future. We
will lose ourselves in the flight and forget about
takeoff and landing. And even while we are still
in midair you can go back to the topless bar and I
will abort and free-fall into a martini glass nicely
chilled by the pedantic Patrick.*

What about the mission?

Forget about the mission.

And the bombing?

*Forget about the bombing. Unless we are
attacked peremptorily by the forces of colonial
expansionism.*

Of course. You're the pilot. That's your job.

That's my job. And it isn't just a job. Except in a 747, which is like a Paris bus with wings. And you?

Me?

You can be a painting strapped into the navigator's seat. If you like. That way you'll be safe.

I don't mind being safe for a while.

22 ✦

Love stops the clock and familiarity winds it up, double speed. Happiness is newness, and, as time passes, all the shortcomings, all the failings of character, pile on top of each other in a rush to push those first moments aside. It was always the same, from the first kiss of adolescence to the lingering, ravenous embrace of middle age, and the pilot knew that what he was doing was forlorn and hopeless even while he was doing it. He knew that when he got on the plane the next day it would be over and done with, a photograph cast to the wind. There wasn't even a photograph this time; he had destroyed the evidence in advance.

The Pigalle Girl had been angry, and now she was afraid. She asked herself whether the pilot was playing a game with her, to test her. Or was he serious when he said that they should forget about the mission, that she could go back to the bar and resume her life? She didn't want to lose him, the thought of never seeing him again put the fear of God in her, but if she were honest with herself, she knew that it was over too. Why had everything become so serious all of a sudden?

She remembered when she had met the pilot, six months earlier, and she remembered all the time they had spent together, never thinking for a moment that anything would have to be discussed. Why did things always have to be discussed?

They walked away from the restaurant and into the courtyard of the Louvre, and the pilot held the Pigalle Girl's hand tightly and more tightly, so that she asked him not to. They stepped onto the Pont des Arts, and they stood looking upriver, following one of the bateaux mouches as it slid under the Pont Neuf and disappeared behind the Île de la Cité, and they both felt better knowing that it might end, for, in ending, they found the beginning again, a time when each word was a new word, each idea a new idea, each touch of skin a new touch.

They had stood there together before, and they remembered. The pilot held the Pigalle Girl, and he felt her body underneath her clothes. And the Pigalle Girl felt the pilot against her. They kissed, and the waves slapped against the piers of the bridge, the tide hurrying past them out to sea, and a man behind them played a guitar and sang badly.

The pilot felt good and fresh, the martinis sending shivers through his body as he looked out to Paris and as he looked into his girl's eyes. The Pigalle Girl smiled at him and nothing else mattered, even though every glimpse of her could be the last. This is infatuation, not love, he said to himself. But where's the harm in that? All things created need to be re-created at one time or another.

They carried on walking, into the Latin Quarter and along the rue de Seine. They came to a hotel with an American name, and the pilot told the Pigalle Girl it was a sign they had to follow.

You're over the limit, pilot.

I'm not even halfway so, he replied.

The man at the desk was kind and enthusiastic, and he showed them to the room at the top, which he thought most appropriate, for it was clear that he was accustomed to couples checking in for the afternoon.

We don't have television, he said, as they rode in the elevator.

The Pigalle Girl giggled and the pilot feigned anger. No television, no deal. I haven't come all this way not to watch television.

The room was simple and clean, and it was a fresh start with fresh sheets. The Pigalle Girl lay naked on the bed and the pilot made love to her as he had done the first time, before they made jokes about flying to places. He forgot about every thought he had ever had, he forgot about the past and the future, and the timelessness of love and desire, and an afternoon fueled by martinis came to save him through the dry skin of his girl. When he pushed himself inside her, drew her legs around him, clasped her at the shoulders, and kissed her breasts, he was both reduced and elevated to all that had been lost within him, and he realized that in losing himself to her, he had been given a glimpse of eternity, or at least a timelessness he had no longer thought possible.

All the pain and suffering of a distant war and a distant peace fell away like the thick vapor trail of an F-111 banking harshly to the right and upward, and he gazed in wonderment as the sky claimed it, rending it apart and absorbing it into the forgiving mass of cloud that seconds earlier he had hardly even noticed. The old fighter jet slipped over the horizon, and the pilot slipped with it.

23 ⚮

The pilot looked around the room. He had awoken and his girl lay asleep in his arms. He lit a cigarette and stared at the wallpaper of this, a new and fresh place from which to stop and start.

He now noticed that the paper that covered the walls also covered the ceiling, and that the pattern, a lavish garden of perennials leading to the same fading chateau, was everywhere around him. He noticed the join in the paper, yet he could not find any instance of the pattern jarring or breaking up, even by the most humble of fractions. He asked himself how anyone could have wallpapered all four walls and ceiling without disrupting so much as a petal or a stem, and he resolved to prove that such a feat was illusory. He followed the lines of the wallpaper seeking out a discrepancy, a jolt, the smallest aberration

*that might concur with human fallibility, yet he
could not hear so much as a whisper of discord
in the garden that surrounded them. He sighed
and lit a cigarette, and the Pigalle Girl awoke
with one eye first, then the other.*

Qu'est-ce qui se passe?

*We have no television. But we are lying amidst
a miracle.*

Miracle?

*Yes, girl. I knew when I saw this hotel from
the street it was special.*

It's the Alabama.

*Apart from the name. Look around you, girl.
Someone has wallpapered all four walls and the
ceiling and there isn't even a join.*

What do you mean, a join?

*He managed to get the pattern to work with
each new length of paper. This room should be
in the Louvre.*

I was dreaming.

So was I.

I won't tell you what I was dreaming.

*Good. Otherwise it'll be spoiled. Like a wish.
We shouldn't talk any more.*

*The pilot stubbed out his cigarette and played
with the Pigalle Girl's skin. He knew that he
was in a garden that was seamless and unbro-
ken in the tiniest detail, and he wanted to keep
it to himself, just as he wanted to keep his girl
to himself. He played with her and he touched
her body with his fingers, tracing lines backward and forward, over her stomach and her
hip and back again. He touched her nipples, and
he watched her carefully as he moved his finger*

down to her thighs. He circled for a while, up one thigh, down the other, and then he touched her between her legs, placing the tip of his finger on her clitoris and pressing it gently, turning it almost imperceptibly in the tiniest of circles. Her eyes closed more tightly, and he looked down at her as she came, her mouth opening and closing, her head turning from side to side.

24 ✧

The spider's web hung limply above his head, pushed by a sudden breeze. He looked below the window and saw another web. It was neat and perfect, like a drawing, and the spider was trapped within it. The spider had consumed neither drink nor drugs nor nicotine, nor anything else that might have upset the manufacture of its web, which was more like a drawing than a real web, so perfect did it seem in all its detail. The spider was abstemious and had never put a leg wrong but was now dead, having probably died of boredom or perfection or both of these things, and the web was useless now, all the work that had gone into it was for nought except as an object of aesthetic and symbolic interest to the poet.

The old fighte* slipped ove* the ho*izon, and the pilot slipped with it.

And the dead spider swayed slightly as Fear opened the window to let the stranger of a breeze into the room. The telephone rang, and it was Harm to say that he hadn't gone on his trip after all and wouldn't go until Fear paid him back the money he owed him. Fear listened to the message by bending down and placing his ear to the lid of the suitcase, and then he sat upright again at his desk so that the sound of Harm floated away to another part of the room, another part of his mind, shutting off the voice so that the Pigalle Girl would be able to respond in peace to the pilot's caresses.

The pilot lay to one side, his prick as hard as it could be, and the Pigalle Girl held it gently, bringing it to her mouth and touching its tip with her tongue and cupping his balls with the palm of her other hand, an act of love that would automatically please the pilot and that would please Madame Jaffré and that would please all the pilots and bank managers of the world and anyone else who might buy the book and respond to a simple love story as they lay in a thousand hotel rooms waiting for the sun to come up or go down or perhaps stay where it was.

Yes, I made love to a woman, said the Pigalle Girl. I made her come with my fingers and I kissed her on the lips and she touched me all over. And there was a man there too who wasn't a pilot, and he made love to me while the woman kissed him and touched him. And then she made love to him and I touched her too, and afterward we were tired and we slept for a while and I never saw them again.

Was it a dream?

I can't remember. I can only remember you.

That's not true. But as long as we are

surrounded by the wallpaper garden we can allow it to be true. As for me, you don't have to remember me, I'm here with you, in the garden.

But I do remember you. This is a memory we are making. It is the past and I am looking back at it, I am watching you and me as we hold each other, because it is the last time and, even if it isn't, it is better to think it is.

What do you mean, girl?

Every time is the last time from now on. That way, we won't wreck it. And when your plane crashes into the future, like you once said it would, I will be below, remembering. It's fine. That's the way it is. And there's nothing we can do about it.

We can still escape.

There is no escape. We have watched each other, we have seen each other from close up and from afar, and all that we did lies between us, a barrier as wide and as deep as the deep blue sea.

25 ✸

Fear had put the Pigalle Girl and the pilot in the seamlessly wallpapered room at the Alabama because that was the room he had shared with the Pigalle Girl on the one night they had spent together.

He had met her at the Armistice and bought her champagne, which the waiter had put on the tab. And he had taken her to the Alabama because his friend Brandt worked there at night and had slipped him a key for nothing. The

Pigalle Girl had been drunk and he had taken advantage of her, but he also knew that she had needed him for her own reasons, too.

Fear had walked into the Armistice late in the evening, having dined with Agostini at the brasserie on the rue des Ecoles. He had spent the day with Agostini, and Agostini had invited him out for dinner afterward.

Agostini had been commissioned to take photographs of a model wearing lingerie in a hotel room. He needed someone to act as an extra, and he had asked Fear if he wanted to do it.

What do I have to do, Agostini?

You just have to act yourself, Fear.

Fear went to the Ritz early in the morning and waited in a suite on the top floor while people arrived to set up the lights and rearrange the furniture. Agostini gave various instructions and chatted to the model while she was being made up by a short man with an earring and a speech impediment. He took Fear aside.

Just sit down and relax over there, Fear. Have some coffee or something. I'll tell you what you have to do when the time comes. This isn't very well paid, I'm afraid. It's editorial.

Editorial?

You know. For the magazine. But don't worry. I'll take you out for dinner tonight. And you get a thousand francs.

Thanks, Agostini. Do I get it in cash?

Sure. We'll find some cash. What we're doing here is a sort of film noir story. That's what all the magazines are doing at the moment.

Why are they all doing the same thing?

Don't ask questions, Fear. We haven't got time. You're a sort of gangster. Marlene is a top model, she's going to be really big. They're going to put her in the next James Bond movie.

Where does she come from?

Kiev, I think. Somewhere like that.

She's so tall. How can a woman be that tall without being a freak?

Keep your voice down, Fear. OK?

It took them two hours to set up the first shot, and when the time came, Fear was positioned beside the model with a gun in his hand given to him by a technician.

Hope it's not loaded, Fear said, pointing it at the girl as he had been told to do.

Someone had better check, the girl said, moving away from Fear. Who is this guy? Is he an actor?

Sure he's an actor, Marly. Will someone check the gun again, please? Agostini said, turning to one of the technicians.

Of course it's not loaded, said the technician.

But I want it double-checked, said Agostini.

Look, if someone doesn't check it right now, I'm leaving, said Marly.

The technician took the gun from Fear and fired it into the air. Nothing happened.

You see?

OK. Let's go. Now Fear, hold Marly around the neck and place your hand over her mouth, pointing the gun at her neck with your other hand.

Fear did as he was requested. He's messing up my makeup, Agostini, said Marlene.

You don't have to do it for real, Fear. Just act. OK?

And there he stood, acting as if he were holding the girl in his arm and pointing the gun at her neck. Agostini started taking pictures and seemed pleased with what he was doing, complimenting Fear and Marlene for the pose they had struck together. Fear felt the coldness of the model and her disinterest in him as he pressed the muzzle of the automatic against her neck and felt her body against his. They were frozen together in a corner of the hotel suite, blinded by the lights, which sent a bead of sweat from Fear's temple onto the girl's shoulder. While Fear was acting, she recoiled as if he really were threatening her, so that the expression on her face became one of genuine surprise and panic, which Agostini thought perfectly appropriate.

Fear spent the day in the hotel suite having his picture taken in various poses. He was tied up to a chair with his back to Marly, who was on another chair, and he was told to lie down on the floor, pretending to be dead. Agostini kept on revising the lighting arrangements and taking roll after roll of film of the model kneeling on the floor and Fear lying there in the middle of the room next to her. The technicians moved back and forth, shifting the lamps, adding colored gels to them and then removing them, touching up Marlene's makeup and flicking powder from Fear's collar that had fallen from Marlene's face as she bent down in an attitude of shock and concern. Fear was exhausted, having gone to bed late and arisen early to work on his Elka Saga, and he fell asleep as everyone administered to the scene. He woke up with a start to find Marlene bending over him.

What's happening? Where am I? he cried.

It's OK, Fear. Don't worry. We'll be done in a minute, said Agostini.

Who is this guy? Is he for real? asked Marlene.

He's a poet in real life, Marly. You like poetry, don't you?

So, he's not an actor.

He's a character actor. That's what we needed for this.

But he could have killed me.

26 ⚔

So, at the end of the day, Agostini took Fear out for dinner, along with some of the others who had worked on the fashion shoot. And after dinner, Fear took his thousand francs from Agostini, who told him he had done a good job.

I didn't do anything, Agostini. Is that a good job?

That's a good job, Fear.

Fear walked around the quarter with his thousand francs, feeling richer than he had in weeks. The money burned a hole in his pocket, and he walked over to a cocktail bar he knew to see if any of his friends were there. He wanted to buy them a drink, but they had either left or were coming later, so he sat at the bar and had a martini, chatting to the barman about life and Paris and women and what he had done that day to earn a thousand francs.

Was she beautiful, Fear? asked the barman.

She was big.

I like big women, said the barman.

Where are the boys? asked Fear.

They're around.

An hour or so later the boys arrived, and Fear bought them drinks because they were always buying him drinks and it was his turn. They still wanted to buy him drinks even though he insisted, so when they had finished drinking and talking, Fear took the barman aside and paid the bill. Now he only had a few francs left, and he didn't want the boys to start paying for him, so he took his leave. It was two o'clock.

Why are you leaving now, Fear? Have you got a date?

Fear stepped out of the bar and headed toward the rue de Buci, feeling the effect of the wine at dinner and the martinis. He felt good, as good as he had done for a while, and his drunkenness flitted from his head to his heart to his stomach like a butterfly that couldn't make up its mind where to land. It wasn't quite spring but he could see the trees were in bud, and he knew that soon enough Paris would be a different place again.

He stopped in at the Armistice for a nightcap and took a table in a corner. Seated at another table was a girl, alone, reading a newspaper and drinking what could have been cognac. Fear asked the waiter to bring him a bottle of champagne because he knew he would be able to put it on the tab and because he was attracted to the girl and thought that if there were a bottle of champagne at hand he might be able to persuade her to join him. He could say it was his birthday.

Ask the young woman if she would like a drink, Fear told the waiter when he brought the bottle.

The waiter walked over to the girl, and the girl turned her head in Fear's direction. Fear tried to look less drunk than he felt, and the resultant smile was probably more grotesque than appealing. He stopped smiling and as soon as he had done so, the girl smiled at him.

It's your birthday?

It was, yes, said Fear, as he could never lie, only bend the truth occasionally.

Happy birthday, then, said the girl, raising the glass the waiter had filled for her.

Fear asked her whether he could join her at her table, and she consented. They drank the champagne together and gave reasons as to why they were alone.

I'm a poet, said Fear.

And I'm in love with a pilot.

So, where's the pilot?

He's in the air.

Makes sense. When's he landing?

I don't know. He took off yesterday and I will never see him again.

Is it always like that?

How do you mean?

Well, do you always tell yourself you will never see him again when he takes off?

No. Just now.

That's too bad.

He's jealous of me but I am faithful. And he has a wife. I am his mistress, and he is in the air heading back to his wife.

Perhaps you should be unfaithful to him. Might make you feel better.

With whom? With you?

I didn't want to use myself as an example.

When the bottle was empty, Fear thanked the waiter and gave him the couple of francs remaining in his pocket as a tip. The bar was closing, and Fear opened the door for the girl. They walked together onto the boulevard so that the girl could get a taxi. There were no taxis waiting, so Fear said he would call for one from the Alabama. The girl was feeling the effect of the brandy and the champagne, and Fear held her around the shoulder as they walked. When they reached the Alabama, he stopped her in the street and kissed her. She kissed him in return and they held each other tightly, as if waiting on the deck of a sinking ship for the sea to swallow them. Then he took her by the hand and led her to the hotel.

If Brandt's there, then this really is my birthday, he thought.

27 ⚸

Fear and the Pigalle Girl took the room with the seamless wallpaper in which Fear would put the Pigalle Girl and the pilot three months later. But nothing that happened between the Pigalle Girl and the pilot happened between the Pigalle

Girl and Fear, because Fear had had too much to drink and because he felt a cad for taking advantage of the Pigalle Girl, even though drunkenness usually served to dampen his conscience.

He felt sorry for the Pigalle Girl and the pilot, and even though he had been told that the pilot had a wife and was unfaithful to his mistress, he couldn't make love to the girl — even if he had been able. Or was he just making excuses, disguising his inability to make love with moral rectitude? Was he lying to himself?

Whatever the reasons or motives or lack of motives, Fear found himself lying in bed with the Pigalle Girl while the Pigalle Girl lay naked beside him, fast asleep. He looked at the Pigalle Girl's body and he thought about making love to her and about what it would be like and then he stared upward to the ceiling, following the pattern of wallpaper that had been pasted up by a master gardener whose ancestor had probably laid out the gardens of Versailles and Luxembourg and various others too labyrinthine to mention. Then he too fell asleep.

Naturally, upon awakening, there was the chance they would make love. Hangovers usually heightened Fear's sexual appetite, but when he looked at the Pigalle Girl lying naked beside him, he decided to abandon any attempt at seduction. To mitigate the traces of guilt that edged his hangover like the rim of a cheap wine glass, he elected forthwith to become something he felt had been lacking in him since leaving Gisèle a few months earlier: a gentleman.

He got up from the bed and drew a bath for the Pigalle Girl, and he went downstairs to get some coffee and croissants. When he returned to the room, the Pigalle Girl was seated in the bath, clutching her legs with her hands, her shoulders hunched, staring ahead of her into the space that was her heart.

Fear laid out the breakfast on the table in the room and lit a cigarette. He had bought a newspaper to check up on the racing, and he waited for the Pigalle Girl to appear from the bathroom. They had breakfast together and they felt relaxed in each other's company, talking about horses and Paris and spring, which seemed more imminent that morning than it had the evening before.

Fear went into the bathroom and washed his face, smoothing back his hair with his fingers. He looked down at the bathtub and at the water still in it and he was astonished by the clarity of it, as if no one had used it all. It was more like the line from a poem than the residue of a simple act of cleanliness by a woman more beautiful than he could ever imagine. Then he went back into the room and kissed the Pigalle Girl politely on the cheek.

They said not one more word to each other. They walked out into Paris, and Fear took the Pigalle Girl to the taxi stand and waited with her for a taxi to appear. When the taxi came, he opened the door for her. She stepped into it, opened the window, and looked up at him for a moment. She smiled.

I don't even know your name, she said.

Fear. And I don't know yours. I just know you come from Pigalle.

Here, she said, scribbling on a cigarette packet and handing it to him. The taxi pulled away and disappeared down the boulevard, around the corner and out of sight, and Fear found himself standing there, quite still, not knowing what to do. He looked down at the palm of his hand and stared at the cigarette packet. Her telephone number was clearly marked. But she hadn't thought to add a name to it.

PART IV

28 ⚘

The master and I are in conversation. He has dismissed Win and Wip with a wave of his hand and they are gone for now, behind the screen door at the far end of the room.

I hope you don't mind my saying, Amor, that I find women a distraction. That, of course, is your function. The more beautiful, the greater the distraction. Do you find Win and Wip beautiful?

Yes.

They have been kind to you?

Yes.

They are nymphomaniacs, both of them. I trust they didn't attempt to molest you.

No, Master.

The master smiles. I have drawn upon Wip occasionally, especially in one of my more recent haikus. I asked her to sit for me, and I stared into her eyes. I instructed her to stop giggling while I worked, and I separated her from Win, for when the two of them are together their telepathic chatter is even more distracting than their beauty. Her giggling went on unabated, however. And with reason, for, once again, I had confused them and was drawing my inspiration not from Wip but from her sister.

What is in a name? the master says. Had I confused their names, or their faces? What difference did it make? Does the poet draw from personality or from appearance? For me, the twins symbolize the poet's dilemma between involvement and abstraction.

It is only through the visual that I achieve an understanding of all things, continues the master. Were I to be born in your age I would take photographs, which I consider the most profound and lingering of art forms — profound because it invites a degree of observation entirely lacking in compromise, lingering because of its unequivocal demand for perfection. To successfully frame in a rectangle what nature has provided in a circle is to appreciate and understand the elemental beauty of existence. Writing, a thousand years hence, will surely have become redundant. The only masters will be those capable of holding a camera correctly.

The photographer is greatly respected in our age, master. And the best paid.

This does not surprise me. And poets? Do they still exist?

Yes. But they find it hard to earn a living, because so few people read their work.

Of course. This is the age of words. Yours is the age of images. If I were to live in the twentieth century, I would spend my time looking, in much the same way as I do now, but I would express myself in pictures rather than hieroglyphs. I would leave my brush and my ink and my rice paper where they belonged, on this table, waiting for another age to appear, for another master to ponder the relevance and mystery of artistic creation, and I would take up the camera and attempt what I consider essentially to be a paradox, to distill from the world around me my own inner aesthetic. Meanwhile, I am here and this is all I have with which to work — along with Win and Wip, whose beauty and incorrigible giggling so amuse and so infuriate me. Which do you prefer, by the way?

It's hard to say.

Because you can't tell them apart?

No, because I haven't made up my mind.

I don't believe you. They have fooled you. As they have fooled me. Perhaps it is they who are the masters, we who are the slaves to their invention.

29 ⋈

The ability to abstract oneself from the moment is not given to all. It can be dangerous. People have been run over remembering a dream and never lived to explain why it was that they walked when they should have waited.

Salt crossed the boulevard, the portable telephone affixed to his ear like a shell. Pedestrians waiting at the lights watched him as he missed a car, then a bus, then a taxi. When he reached the other side he stopped, and while he stood there the lights changed and the pedestrians who had been waiting crossed the boulevard, catching up with him and drawing him into their wake. He continued on his way but after a while realized he was on the wrong side of the boulevard, so he crossed over again, all the time talking into his telephone. He had been looking for Fear all day, dialing numbers and wondering whether he was still in Paris. He had called Fear's room and he had tried Information, and he still had no idea where he might be.

Salt had made a fortune ten years earlier by producing a film based on an obscure novel from the 1950s, the rights for which he had appropriated after coming across the volume at a *bouquiniste* on the quai des Célèstins. It told the story of an English civil servant in India who is forced through circumstance to run a maharajah's kingdom after the heir presumptive and his father are killed in a freak accident (Rolls Royce, level crossing). The tale was fourth-rate Rudyard Kipling, but the demand for nostalgic films concerning the British Raj being apparently insatiable, Salt had succeeded in marketing the finished product to perfection. Did not the whole Western world wish to share in England's illustrious past, coupled with tremendous acting, fantastic costumes, and no less than three original steam locomotives?

Salt had vainly attempted to repeat this success ever since by searching for ideas of similar potential. None had worked, yet he still clung to the superstitious belief that the English were the best writers for his purposes, and he sought them out with a conviction that impressed his wife and amused his competitors.

He had been led to Fear by a man who worked in the English bookshop in Saint-Germain. Fear had once written a novel set in Portugal, and the man in the shop recommended it to the rather nervous American, who explained he was looking for a story of commercial interest. He read the blurb on the cover and the first three chapters before buying it. He was subsequently introduced to the author by the salesman when Fear happened to be standing in the same bookshop two weeks later.

Comedy. Tragedy. I don't care, he said to Fear. But something pertinent to the nineties.

Salt never quite understood Fear's love story, but he liked the idea of shifting the setting from 1920s Los Angeles to 1990s Paris, and of Buster Keaton's wife getting lost in Disneyland while Buster conducted an affair with a supermarket checkout girl in Paris. He didn't show it to the Hollywood studios, because he knew they wouldn't understand it either. In fact, he forgot all about it for a while, concentrating on other projects that he thought more commercially viable, but in which he lost interest as time passed and financial backing became more scarce. The day before, however, he had heard from a French television network that they wished to proceed with the project and he now had funds at his disposal to make it.

Salt was no longer a wealthy man. In the past, with a good lawyer, he had never had any problem in dealing with authors who made claims on their work. But it was different in the nineties. Salt wanted to buy Fear out by paying him the 500 dollars he owed him, along with the $10,000 he had promised him when the film went into production, and he couldn't proceed until he had settled the matter. He was concerned he might be sued by Fear afterward, so he had prepared a contract that excluded the author from any further benefits from the film, confident that a quick buyout would appeal to him.

So this was why Salt strode the boulevard, crossing it backward and forward and making calls on his portable telephone, dialing Fear's old number again to check that no one knew of his whereabouts, and trying to think of anyone else he could call who might know where he was.

He was standing at an intersection further along the boulevard, still trying to rid himself of the one impediment that held back his reputation, when he realized all of a sudden that he had stepped off the pavement and was in the path of an oncoming cyclist. The cyclist veered to the right to avoid him and struck a woman pushing a baby stroller across the street.

I'll call an ambulance, he shouted, turning to the woman and the cyclist, who was now lying in the gutter.

The cyclist looked up at him plaintively and Salt hovered for a moment before dialing the emergency number on his telephone. Two minutes! he shouted, continuing along the boulevard and turning back to the cyclist, who had now gained the safety of the sidewalk.

Then he called his office.

Make a note of it, Françoise. Minor traffic accident brings a man and a woman together. Woman holds the man in her arms as they wait for an ambulance. Their eyes meet. They fall in love. At first sight. Make it one love story in a thousand others set in contemporary Paris, all connected by haphazard incidents, the through-line being traffic.

An ambulance screamed past, its blue light flashing, its siren breaking the noise of the traffic as it headed down the boulevard. Salt followed its passing and then looked up to the sky, the telephone at his ear.

A woman is heartbroken. She decides to throw herself off the Pont Neuf. She jumps just as her lover appears on the bridge and runs toward her. The man races to the other side of the bridge so he can beat the tide, dive in, and save her. But he never makes it. He is run over by a car. We now realize that the woman didn't drown at all. She fell onto a coal barge.

And then, quite suddenly, he put the telephone back in his pocket and marched off into the distance.

30 ❧

The Pigalle Girl looked up to the ceiling and remembered being in the same room before with the Englishman who hadn't made love to her, just drawn a bath for her and gone to get breakfast.

What's up, girl?

Nothing.

I don't believe you.

Let's go.

The pilot and the Pigalle Girl got dressed in silence and they took the elevator down to the lobby.

Sorry about the television, said the man at reception.

What television? asked the pilot.

They stepped out into the street and walked across the boulevard and up the rue de Seine.

Let's go to the gardens. They're around here somewhere, aren't they? said the pilot, taking the Pigalle Girl's hand.

They turned to the right, toward place Saint-Sulpice, and then past the huge church that filled a city block to their left.

Didn't you take me there once to see some paintings?

The Delacroix.

Let's go and see them again.

I don't want to see them again. I want to see new things.

The fountain created a stream of cool air above their heads as they walked through the square, and the Pigalle Girl stopped to put her hand into the water and dab a few drops on her forehead. The pilot kissed her and looked up to the church, and then he took the Pigalle Girl by the shoulder and kissed her again.

Paris is always like a dream to me, he said. Like a picture. How do people live in a place that looks like a picture?

They are used to it, captain. They are used to Paris and Paris is used to them. I walk through it without noticing sometimes. I belong to it yet I could leave tomorrow and never come back; and if I did return when I was old, nothing would have changed. There would just be more boutiques and less bookshops.

When they reached the gardens they walked past people playing chess and tennis, further up. Tourists took photographs of each other, and children rode on Shetland ponies. At the top, near rue Vavin, they looked at the fruit trees that had been carefully trained in a crisscross pattern.

It's exactly like the wallpaper, the pilot said. Only here there's not even a join in the paper.

It was late afternoon, and the sun cast shadows across the pathways as they headed toward the round pond. Small sailboats lay becalmed near its center, and the pilot helped a child to bring in a yacht with the aid of a stick. The children stood apart from the adult world, and the adult world watched, remembering its own childhood, a ship becalmed, just beyond its reach. The pilot and the Pigalle Girl still held hands as they walked, but they didn't say anything to each other, they simply thought along parallel lines of meaning and, as they did so, they wondered what the other might be thinking.

What are you thinking? asked the Pigalle Girl.

I was just going to ask you the same thing.

They were both glad to step out of the gardens. The Pigalle Girl resented them for their perfection and neatness. She felt they had dulled her senses; she thought them too beautiful and not suited to the disorder in her mind. She didn't want to see families and children and lovers holding hands and kissing, all content with their lives, organized, married, settled, secure, as carefully laid out as the flower beds and the espalier fruit trees. She wanted to be elsewhere, away from Paris, by the sea where she had once gone *with a man whose name she forgot or up in the air, above the clouds, where there was nothing to impede the view. The man had wanted to marry her and she had laughed at him. How cruel she had been to laugh; her laughter now rang in her ears as she looked up into sky and saw the emptiness that was her future.*

It's cocktail time, said the pilot. We're late.

31 ⚜

They headed down the boulevard and toward Saint-Germain-des-Prés. The pilot knew that it would be difficult to find anyone who could mix a martini, and he suggested going to the Ritz or Harry's Bar, but the Pigalle Girl knew a place where a friend of hers worked, near Les Halles, so they went there instead.

The bar was American in style, and the pilot knew that he wouldn't have to spend so much time explaining how things should be done.

Are you always on a mission, captain?

Not always. Sometimes I'm resting. It depends.

On what?

On who I'm with and whether or not I've recently completed a mission. The law states that one should rest between missions. It is a law of common sense, not of averages, and it is directly related to optimum strike rate.

But even when you are not on a mission you are still trying to find the perfect martini.

I've been looking for it for years. I nearly

found it a few years ago, but it slipped from my fingers.

What do you think of this place?

It's like America. Which one is your friend?

The girl. Don't worry. You don't have to be jealous.

Even though you sleep with women too.

That was a joke.

She's pretty.

Now I'm jealous.

You don't get jealous.

She is pretty. Shall I ask her to mix your martini for you?

Can women mix martinis?

Let's see.

Tell her I want it straight up with a twist. Can you do that in French?

What does it mean?

Try it in American first.

The Pigalle Girl ordered the martini, and her friend understood how to do it. She brought the martini to the pilot and placed it in front of him.

Any good? asked the Pigalle Girl.

The pilot produced a small Havana from the pocket of his shirt and lit it with a match. He exhaled a small cloud of smoke above the bar, and then he took a sip of the martini. The martini slid down his throat and reached the point it was supposed to reach for him to know whether or not it was any good. The nicotine from the cigar went elsewhere, toward his head, meeting the martini taste and acknowledging it politely. His body responded to what it was being given and to the lovemaking that had preceded the martini and the cigar an hour or so earlier, which still made his legs feel weak and his loins tingle.

The moment was full and there was neither past nor future to get in its way; it rose like a jet moving upward away from the enemy into a corner of sky. He was away from danger and away from everything he had ever known, and the Pigalle Girl seemed like a stranger to him, so fresh was this moment suspended by God from the ceiling of the American-style bar in the heart of Paris.

The martini? Not bad.

32 ⚶

The Pigalle Girl spoke perfect English because the pilot didn't speak French, and Fear didn't want language to interfere with what he was saying about how things were between them. The Pigalle Girl spoke better English than Gisèle, even though Gisèle had benefited from a complete university education, augmented by the set of BBC tapes she had bought by mail order, and even though the Pigalle Girl had never done anything except work in a topless bar in Pigalle, where the English she learned was conversational and to the point and usually about Paris and the correct way to mix martinis. But that was the way Fear wanted it. And he didn't think it would bother Madame Jaffré one bit, or anyone else, for that matter.

Fear much preferred the Pigalle Girl to any of the other women he had been with, and he was pleased that she was cleverer than Gisèle, because when he thought about it, he didn't like Gisèle at all now and he was only fooling himself when he decided that there was still room in his heart for her or for anyone else. Gisèle had wanted him to change into a better person, and he had only become worse, *worser,* in her eyes, which is what he had wanted to achieve to spite her, to prove to her that you couldn't change people into what you wanted, that it was a waste of time trying and you should probably find someone else.

The language, in any case, was unimportant, just as most of the other details, taken separately, were unimportant. Life was not a jigsaw puzzle, not every piece had to be in place or even form part of the same picture; neither was it like a French garden nor the seamless wallpaper in which the Pigalle Girl and Fear, and the Pigalle Girl and the pilot, had passed time together. Life was a delightful mess that required faith, and fate, to sustain it, for a mess needed sustaining just as much as a fruit tree that had been turned into something that looked less like a tree and more like an illustration of the parallelogram of forces stuck to a fence.

No, it was not the language but the tone of the conversation that told of the sparring and the loving that went on between the Pigalle Girl and the pilot as they seesawed between tenderness and resentment and regret, knowing that, because they had started to think of its impossibility, their affair was doomed as all things are doomed that need to be considered and reconsidered. But they were still in love, and what was important was to describe their love story, which by its sheer hopelessness became a great love story, despite the fact that it was unlikely anyone would be really interested in a Boeing 747 pilot with a wife and two children in Anaheim or a girl who worked in a topless bar around the corner from place de Clichy.

Fear looked through the window, and the ball bounced across the courtyard. One of the Arab boys ran past Eton's window and kicked it back toward the opposite end. A woman cried out to his right, the Arab boy laughed, a truck could be heard racing down the street, and the sun rose higher in the sky, making Fear wipe his brow as if he had undertaken a journey and stopped for a moment in the shade somewhere to rest.

He got up from his table and poured himself a pastis, and then he stood by the window. Eton was still playing the piano; he would play it all day and stop only when he was tired. He pressed the keys and made notes, composing stories that went off in all directions, stories of love and war and the greatest battle ever fought by man. The ball bounced back and forth along the courtyard, occasionally hitting the wall of his apartment, and Eve sat upstairs in her studio working on whatever it was she worked on so hard. Above her, the man who always had a beer in his hand sat beside the window looking at something Fear couldn't see, and all the courtyard, of which Fear was a part without fully realizing it, seemed to be heading, like a ship, on a steady course laid out for it by a brave yet prudent helmsman. The sky was clear, the sea was calm, and as Fear thought about the love between the Pigalle Girl and the pilot, and the story that grew from it, he felt complete, at peace with himself, like someone who has been given exactly what he wants for his birthday.

The telephone rang and it was Madame Jaffré. Her voice was gentle. Was everything all right? Did he have enough money to buy paper, or would he care to pass by the bank, and she would give him a ream, along with some spare pencils?

He drank his pastis and moved back to his desk and he stared down at the spider's web with the spider still stuck, so neatly, within it.

That's what perfection brings. Aiming for it is more satisfying than getting it, he said aloud to the spider, even though the spider was dead and didn't necessarily understand English.

33 ❧

The evening was past, the martinis were a memory of perfection unattained, and the Pigalle Girl lay in the pilot's arms looking out through the window. The neon light below sent patterns across the ceiling, a message, thrown upward and refracted through the thickened windowpane, which she could stare at for hours if she wanted. She never tired of it; it comforted her when the pilot was away, and it comforted her now as she lay close to him, knowing that he would leave in a few hours and perhaps never come back.

The pilot was asleep. Who knows what he is dreaming? she thought. Soon, he would be gone and she would be alone again. She would return to the topless bar and get her job back, and she would find another man to sleep with so that she would be able to forget about the pilot and take revenge on him and on all the other pilots in the world who flew in circles dreaming of lovers they might have in faraway places.

She knew what would happen. She would serve a businessman from Stuttgart or Sheffield or some other place beginning with S that she had never heard of, perhaps she would meet him after work and let him make love to her, and even though that would make her a pute, *she would be less of a* pute *than a girl who is taken care of by a pilot who already has a wife in Los Angeles and doesn't allow her to work for a living, who just wants her to be a painting he can look at, like the paintings in the Louvre that show naked women in the salons of wealthy Parisians from another age. Or she would walk the streets of Paris and find a café somewhere and sit in it at a table on her own, and someone, a complete stranger with kind eyes and a warm laugh, would offer to buy her a drink.*

She had to change her life back to what it had been before, because in that different life she had more security than in any other. She would have to forget about the pilot forever, and the only way she could think of doing it would be to sleep with another man whose touch and caresses were different and new. No, she wouldn't go

with a man in the bar, she would look for the

man with kind eyes who would think of her as she was, and then one day perhaps take her away to live in a house by the sea where the sky met the horizon in a wavy line of blueness and harmony; he would marry her and they would have children and he would go out to catch fish every morning and sometimes risk his life for her, while she cared for the children and embroidered a prize-winning tapestry describing the history of life and love from silk thread in many colors. Damn it! He can be a plumber for all I care, just so long as he's not a pilot.

The pilot slept. The Pigalle Girl got up from the bed and lit a cigarette. She slipped on her dressing gown and walked over to the window so that the neon caught her face and made her blink. The traffic was heavy on the boulevard; she could see the buses parked near the Moulin Rouge and the tourists spilling out of them, disappearing into the sex shops and the bars. I could be serving them, she thought. I could be making money instead of looking through the window, money that would go toward the cost of a radar on the fishing boat or a new net, as we have decided the old one is finally past repair.

The night filled the Paris air, and the neon flickered, sending its message across the windshields of passing cars and the windows of the buses parked nearby. The city was alive at night, it breathed a different air, more vital, more threatening. The darkness brought meanness; man let go, eased by drink, pushed forward to the dawn by his own malevolence, his own desire for self-destruction. Someone would get stabbed tonight. Someone always got stabbed. The Pigalle Girl remembered seeing a boy running down the street, chased by a man with a knife, and she had watched from a corner as the boy slipped forward, clutching his heart. She had run away, down the hill and away from Pigalle, and she hadn't stopped until she reached the river, washing the thought, the memory, from her mind. Only now it came back, it would never leave her, the thought of the boy gasping for breath and dying for nothing.

She lay back upon the bed and stubbed out her cigarette. The pilot stirred, his dreams turning him first to one side, then the other. She took him in her arms, her heart torn with the betrayal of her thoughts. She no longer wanted to be back in the bar, she wanted to escape with him, up, above, away to a place where Paris was never mentioned and all that she ever was or ever had been was gone, just a shadow on a wall or a ceiling somewhere, shut up within a room within a building on the corner of the boulevard for someone else to look at. She held the pilot tightly, and the pilot opened his eyes. He knew she was afraid, and he put his arms under her dressing gown and felt her body trembling, and he soothed her and comforted her as she thought of Paris and the night and the ghost of a boy lying in the gutter. He drew her closer, pulled her on top of him, and moved her legs apart so that her thighs pressed against his hips. He put his arms over her shoulders, his hands behind her neck and he stared into her sad, brown eyes.

I know what you're thinking, girl. And, whatever it is, you're right. I'm an old veteran, the oldest forty-six-year-old in the history of forty-six-year-olds, and you are young and deserve better than a man who seems only interested in martinis.

But I want you, captain.

I want you. Where shall we go this time?

Let's just fly over the horizon for a while. Even high up we can still see the white horses when there's a gale.

34 ✷

The neon played against her body, a string of letters stretching from her breasts to the shin of her right leg, the upturn of an E *or a* P *kissing the pilot's stomach so that they were both bathed in the message, the same message that caught and attracted those who wandered the boulevard, postponing their dreams and ignoring the dawn that awaited them around the corner with a switchblade.*

The pilot held the Pigalle Girl by the hips, and the Pigalle Girl moved up and down on his prick, her hair falling from her face so that the pilot had to part it with his finger in order to kiss her. The pilot held the Pigalle Girl's buttocks tightly and pushed her up and down, drawing her closer and closer to him so that he could feel her womb and feel everything inside her, and the tightness of her and the smoothness of her made him gasp and cry out to her in the silence of the room, and every nerve and neuron tingled in his body like on a maiden flight in an F-111 only much better, much much better than anything he had felt before. They were miles away from where they had been, and they looked down at what they were doing from a great height, watching and waiting as the pleasure became more intense and the yearning shifted to a muffled panic, desire meeting desire head-on and pushing all else aside.

The Pigalle Girl raised herself from the pilot and held him tightly, and the pilot's heart beat faster and faster as he waited to be inside her again; she drew circles with her finger over his chest and moved her finger downward to tease him. She took him in her mouth and she felt his coming, and then she stopped again and lay on her back. And the pilot entered her and kissed her breasts and her neck, and when he came she came with him in waves on a horizon she could now touch with her hand, a line of forgetting as far from anything as anything could possibly be.

There was no stopover, she said. On this flight.

We diverted and would have ditched but the ground came to rescue us.

It was south but I lost my bearings.

It wasn't south, girl. It was west. But you couldn't tell, as you had an aisle seat.

It's late.

It's early. I can feel it. The neon is fading.

And then the dawn came, appearing from around its corner and scowling at the night, sending it scurrying off into the distance, away to the west, past the outskirts, through La Défense and off through the rest of France to the sea. The fishermen brought in the fruits of their labor to those who had rested, slept, and awoken to make a decent breakfast, steaming café au lait *and* pain au chocolat *drawn from the oven, and the men stood by their catch, smoking cigarettes and cracking jokes about fish and women. There I will be, thought the Pigalle Girl, catching the dawn as it moves slowly west.*

They lay side by side in silence. The pilot stared at the painting on the opposite wall, and the Pigalle Girl looked at the pilot's uniform on a hanger beside it before turning away and sitting up in the bed.

What's the painting?

It's a view from afar. I got it in the market.

Where is it supposed to be?

It's not supposed to be anywhere. It's just a painting. From the south, maybe.

The pilot smiled. He looked at his watch on the bedside table, picked it up, and strapped it onto his wrist. Then he got out of bed and walked over to the painting, and the Pigalle Girl laughed at him.

What's funny?

You look so strange. Naked except for a watch.

I'm superstitious about the watch, he said, laughing with her and looking closer. Looks like a decent sort of place. A place you could go to and be happy in.

You can't go there. It's made up. But you can look at it.

I had better shower. I'm late.

Take off your watch. It'll get wet otherwise.

The pilot went into the bathroom, and the Pigalle Girl sat on the bed, quite still. The light had come up and the neon no longer shone in the room. She walked over to the window and stared out to the boulevard. She closed up the curtains and went back to the bed, and the pilot returned and began to dress. He looked in the mirror on the wall near the doorway as he fastened his tie and put on his jacket. And when he had finished, he stood at the foot of the bed with his hat under his arm.

Do I look stranger now?

You look as if you are going on a mission.

That's how I feel, girl.

What is your mission?

My mission is America because I am angry with it for being in the wrong place. But don't tell anyone. It's a D9.

What's a D9?

A D9 is so classified that no one knows what it is.

I'm on a D9 too.

That's good and proper.

That's my mission.

The pilot sat down on the bed and looked back at the painting before turning to face the Pigalle Girl again. Sometimes I see the world turning in circles, I mean I can actually see it. I see its curvature, its oceans, its mountains, its landscapes. And I see all the cities of the world stuck like pins into it to help the person whose job it is to turn it.

Whose job is it?

That depends on the schedule. It varies according to where you are and what time it is.

And where the dateline falls. It is not fixed. You just take it in turns, do your duty, do what you are told, obey the rules so that once in a while, when the mood takes, you can break them. Just like that.

Like what?

Like that, said the pilot, snapping his fingers.

35 ✤

Fear looked through his window, smoking a cigarette, opening his eyes as if he had never seen the world before, awakening from the night and from the grip of his own bewildered imagination.

For the first time in weeks it had rained, and the cobbles in the courtyard glistened in the first rays of sunlight. Some parts of the courtyard were already dry, others formed puddles in which the fallen leaves of the huge honeysuckle affixed to the opposite wall floated carelessly. The air was fresh and invigorating, and people opened their windows to let it in.

The man who always had a beer in his hand had just appeared from the front door adjacent to Eton and Eve's apartment. He had his dog with him. His face was pale and drawn and unshaven as he marched off to Rocket Street to buy more beer. The night had passed thus, the darkness, the heat and the rain had all come and disappeared, the sun had made its circle, the earth had turned forward or backward or sideways in tune with it, and everything found its place again, restored to a natural order after the chaos of all that was human, all that was good and bad and irrevocable, had interfered with it.

Fear could tell, even from a distance, that the man was hung over and that he was already savoring the beer he would bring back with him and take up to his apartment. He would sit on his windowsill, in exactly the same place, and he would sip at his beer and watch the day pass through the lens of whatever it was he looked through — a pile of bodies, a plane falling from the sky, a cure for the plague, a team of cyclists sweating up a mountain for no other reason than the chance to get there first, or second, or perhaps not at all, all the things that made up the universe and that were then reported on television, for Fear had long since decided that the man watched television as he drank his beer and attended to the needs of his dog.

He sat at his table and put another piece of paper into the roller, blessing Agostini for all the photographs he had ever taken and would ever take, all the girls with smiles on their faces who stood for hours quite still for the camera, all the people who worked for all the glossy magazines ever printed that paid Agostini so that Agostini could sponsor the poetry of Fear and of all the Fears who thought they could write, even when they turned the letters on their typewriters into a coded language of desire that set out to reflect the desire of all and that would lead to astounding commercial success in this, the "pertinent" world of midnineties eroticism.

Bang went the keys, bang went the asterisk,

bang went Fear's heart, and bang went the chord on Eton's piano as Eve stepped out of her studio and set off on a mission of artistic import. And bang went the ball against the window as the Arab boy gave one last kick to it before going to school. The man returned with his beer and his hangover and his smile, which became a smile of irony to anyone who happened to be watching, and his dog followed him, also smiling, for why shouldn't dogs smile too, when it has been proved that they can dream?

What do I know about dogs? What do I know about people? And who was it who said that there is no wrong step, just the next step?

PART V

36 ⚘

I couldn't sleep last night. I have always had difficulty sleeping. Like Nabokov, I am an insomniac. In one of his novels, he describes night as being a giant. He was right.

I poured myself a stiff vodka and tonic and turned on the television. There was a talk show on which two Frenchmen were shouting simultaneously so that, as the camera turned from one to the other, it seemed as though each of them had two contradictory voices. One of them was explaining that even a baker could be an intellectual. It might have been banker. *Boulanger. Banquier.* Well, it's closer in English, of course, but I can be forgiven for confusing the two even in French, for I was tired, if sleepless.

I switched channels. A surprisingly beautiful woman was giving a blow job to a rather dull and disinterested actor. I watched the woman work on the man's prick until he came in her mouth. She was rather good at it — she had obviously had some practice — and the actor became quite animated as he came. He must have enjoyed his orgasm, yet it was clear that he was also acting out his excitement, so it was extremely difficult for me to ascertain the precise extent of his pleasure. This intrigued me for some reason. As he came, he looked up to the ceiling of the studio with his eyes closed, as if, like Saint Paul, he were turning toward God. Frankly, I don't know what God would have thought of it. He made the Garden of Eden. And we made Eve give Adam a blow job on cable television. I liked the girl, though. She turned me on for some reason. Was it because of my recent haiku fantasy, in which the twin geishas made love to me?

While the two Frenchmen continued to argue about whether a baker or a banker could be an intellectual, and about whether language was a help or a hindrance in the delineation of fundamental truths, countless acts of sex and coitus, some real, some imagined, others televised, punctuated the night. I wondered how many couples in Paris made love as I sat there with my vodka and tonic, watching television, and I longed to count myself among their number.

On another channel, two boxers stepped from their respective corners and began fighting. One was short and stocky, the other tall and lean. The short one was Russian, the tall one Algerian. They were evidently the same weight, yet they were vastly different in stature and appearance, which made the fight a true contest between opposites. I am not a sports fan and cannot claim to know much about boxing, but I was fascinated by the struggle that developed between them. It was like an Aesop's fable.

The Russian kept up a good guard, not allowing the Algerian any room to maneuver, but he couldn't reach the Algerian's body, of course, because his arms were too short. This went on for several rounds, the commentator indicating that they were evenly matched in points.

After a while, the Russian grew increasingly frustrated and gave the Algerian a heavy punch below the belt. The Algerian cried out and fell to his knees. When he recovered, he changed his style and his tactics. While he had been content earlier on to dance skillfully around his opponent, he was now goaded into an attack of brute force. He flew out of his corner at the beginning of the last round, still suffering from the blow to his genitals, and punched the Russian so hard in the face that he fell flat on the floor, knocked unconscious.

It was now late and when I switched over, the two French intellectuals were still arguing. There was no more sex on the cable channel, but I thought about the beautiful woman who had given the man the blow job, and I felt aroused as I sipped my vodka and tonic. I touched myself and brought myself to orgasm as I lay on the sofa, and with the last, lingering waves of pleasure it gave me, I fell asleep.

37

Despite feeling tired, I managed to accomplish more work this morning than any other during the last two weeks. I decided to have lunch in my favorite brasserie off the boulevard Saint-Michel to celebrate.

I am now sitting at my table in the corner, watching the waiters as they go about their work. In an alcove, I see the chef's hands as he places a dish on the counter, and I follow the movement of that dish as it is collected by the waiter and transported to an adjacent table. I see the dish move up and down, side to side, avoiding any number of collisions, so that by the time it is set on the table, I can say that it has embarked on and successfully completed a voyage of sorts. The entire proceeding is one that has been repeated again and again through time immemorial, just as it will continue to be repeated into the future, long after I have left my table and gone forever. I look at the waiters, and I think of how they have always done what they are now doing, and I see in the transportation of the dish the transportation of time through the ages, forward into the twenty-first century and backward to the time of Fujiwari no Kintō. The master might have lived one thousand years ago, but to me, the past has the same value, it is in itself ageless, as indefinable as the small pile of dust that has collected below the chef's alcove.

Yes, every act has been repeated and will continue to be repeated; it forms part of the circular nature of existence, from the movement of the chair and the table to the suggestion of an aperitif, the taking of the order to the delivery of the order, the protracted discussion of a suitable wine to the acceptance or rejection of a certain type of cheese or salad or dessert. Why pay money to go to the theater, I find myself asking, when you can come to this brasserie and perform your own lunch?

And the more I think about it, the more I realize that in seeing everything repeated just as it was before I was born, I am the closest I will ever be to eternity, for the simple reason that time itself has been suspended. The clock on the wall turns as if for its own sake and its alone; even it, that barefaced cheek of mahogany, can do nothing to change the timelessness of this brasserie in which I and a million others have sat so many times. It makes very little difference whether the hour hand indicates two o'clock or three o'clock or ten o'clock, for time itself is in the hands of some higher authority, capricious, autocratic, the meek wooden instrument on the wall merely following the rhythms set out for it by those who scurry back and forth, and who have always and will always scurry back and forth, with food and wine and beans and apple tart and anything else anyone might have ordered.

No, the real master in this instance is not God, nor Fujiwari no Kintō, nor the minute hand of the clock, nor that of all the clocks that exist in this world within and outside this brasserie, but the man with the bald pate and the bow tie, polished shoes and permanent shadow to his cheeks, now seen holding a beer mat inverted in the palm of his left hand, the pen in his right deleting the table for four that has just appeared from the street. He shows them to their table and smiles again as he passes me on the banquette to his right.

Tout va bien, Madame?

Oui, Monsieur, I reply. *Comme d'habitude.* 125

38 ❧

In another restaurant, some distance away and over the river, a man in a gray flannel suit registered the tardiness of his lunch partner by looking at his watch and frowning. Just then, Salt burst though the door and hurried over to the table to make his excuses (meeting, traffic, family, parking) before beckoning to the waiter and requesting champagne *tout de suite.*

So, what can you tell me about Fear? asked Salt, as the waiter deposited two glasses on the table.

Fear?

Yes.

I met him once at a dinner. He smashed his head through a window. Or did he throw a bottle through it? I can't remember. He's a poet, if such a thing still exists. He's quite funny. But he's crazy. Like all the English. One of my photographers knows him quite well. You know Agostini?

I've heard of him. He's very successful, isn't he?

Ten thousand dollars a day.

Lot of money in fashion.

Lot of fashion in money.

Well, if you speak to this guy, I need to find out where Fear is. If he's still in Paris.

Oh yes, he's still in Paris. I can get his number.

Good. So what else do you know about him?

Fear?

Yes.

I think he does quite well when he's not being obnoxious and confusing people. Apparently, he's working on a big project for one of the Hollywood studios. Must have a hot agent.

What was the project? Did Arnolfini tell you?

Agostini? Didn't say. That was a few months ago.

He worked for me a few months ago, earlier in the year. But he didn't mention it. Not that he should have, necessarily. There's probably more to him than I thought. I'll have to be careful.

Why?

He wrote a treatment for me. A comedy. The idea is good, and I'm cutting the deal. I just have to square things away with him. That's all. Paperwork, really.

You'll manage that, Salt. You always do.

I've got to make this one work. I don't want any problems.

Don't be so dramatic. You should relax more.

Relax?

Yes. Work out now and then.

I do that already, but it doesn't seem to help.

What about analysis?

Haven't got the time. What about you?

Me? Great.

Did you get that supermarket account you were chasing?

Yes. We used Ulla Eriksson. Agostini did the pictures. And now she's plastered on the side of every bus in Paris. Great pair of legs.

What's that got to do with a supermarket?

Nothing.

I don't understand anything anymore.

127

There's nothing to understand, Salt. You can sell anything with a decent pair of legs.

I know. But vegetables?

Don't think about it. Now, what are you going to have?

Is it my turn or yours?

39 ❧

When Fear awoke, his signet ring was not on the little finger of his left hand but on his right. Then he realized that he was still dreaming, that he had dreamed he had awoken to find his signet ring on the wrong finger. And as he acknowledged the fact, he closed his eyes again, in his sleep. He dreamed several times that he was awake so that when he finally was, he thought he was dreaming. He opened his eyes and he closed them. And then he opened them again. He looked around the room and lit a cigarette, and only when he coughed did he know he was no longer asleep.

It was first light. He made himself some coffee and went over to his table. He worked through the dawn, and as the sun rose, the cobbles in the courtyard began to dry out so that only a patch of wetness remained along the wall below his studio. The words came together in a way that pleased him, and he felt at peace with himself. Nothing stirred, not even the soccer ball, and he wondered when the Arab boy would appear and kick it back across the courtyard.

The pilot had taken his leave of the Pigalle Girl and gone to the airport, and Fear used the dawn to describe the emptiness in the Pigalle Girl's heart as she looked through the window, watching the pilot step out into the boulevard and hail a taxi.

The first taxi didn't stop, so the pilot waited for another, his bag at his side, a cigarette drawn to his mouth, smoke exhaled into the damp summer air of early morning, while the Pigalle Girl thanked the first driver for not stopping, so she could say goodbye once again to the pilot, framing him in her mind as he stood there like a stranger, just a man dressed as a pilot she might have seen one morning as she looked through her window without really noticing.

There was very little traffic, and Paris seemed still, at peace with itself in this corner of the city, just one or two clochards passing by, stopping to look through the rubbish that had collected in the litter bins overnight, and a pair of lovers arm in arm making their way home along the boulevard. A tear fell down the Pigalle Girl's cheek as she looked at the couple, at the pilot, and then at the couple again. And when she looked back, a taxi had finally stopped and the pilot was in the backseat. The taxi pulled away, and the Pigalle Girl turned from the window and lay on the bed. She looked at the landscape painting and tried to lose herself within it, imagining she was far away from Pigalle and Paris and everything else that was familiar to her, but it was too distant, this view of elsewhere, as far from her as anything could possibly be, so she put her face in her hands and closed her eyes tightly for a moment. 129

When she opened her eyes, she looked around the room, so empty now that the pilot had gone and gone forever. There was so little of him left for her to look at, just the coat hanger on the wardrobe door that had held his uniform in place during his stay and the martini shaker on the bedside table. The top of the table was marked with a ring of moisture from the night before, when the shaker had been cold. She picked up the shaker and looked inside. There were still a few drops of martini inside. She lit a cigarette and poured the last of the martini into the captain's glass and drank it carefully, savoring the whiff of cigar smoke that went with it and recoiling from the bitterness of the gin, which she knew had 1 percent vermouth mixed in with it. Then she put the glass back on the bedside table and lay back on the bed, covering herself with the sheet and grasping the pillow with both hands.

The pilot is gone and I will never see him again, she thought. I know it. And that is the way it should be. Everything has a logic to it completely outside our control. Every story has been written for us beforehand, we can cheat if we like, skipping the pages and reading the last chapter, but it doesn't make any difference, we are condemned to live in the present, to lose ourselves in each, faltering moment, and once what is supposed to happen has happened, all we can do is look back and try to capture what we have lost. The last of the martini is gone and there will never be another. Why did he leave his shaker behind? Now he will think about his shaker, he won't think about me, and I was a fool for ever thinking otherwise.

40 ✕

Fear still had some of the money Agostini had given him. Deducting what he had spent on the paper and the pastis and the drinks he'd had in the bar, there were 342 francs left.

He was reaching the end of the love story, but there was still the last chapter to write. He didn't want to rush it; he knew that something else was going to happen but that it would come only with the writing.

He looked down at his work and then stood up from his table to gain a fresh perspective on it. Then he took his money and the last three chapters of his book and stepped out into Rocket Street. He went up to the café and sat at a table, reading through his work and drinking a coffee. He saw Agostini passing by and called out to him.

No, Fear. You're working. I won't disturb you.

Thanks, Agostini. Thanks for everything. For being a photographer. For taking pictures. For buying me paper. And cigarettes. And this coffee. And a meal with a girl that won't necessarily happen but could happen because of the money you gave me. You are the patron saint of all scribblers, and all scribblers swear allegiance to you and are ready to declare war on Germany if necessary.

Why Germany?

Because they are the best fighters and always go down slowly.

You're crazy, Fear. Even when you're drinking coffee.

The coffee winds me up. The pastis slows me down. The writing moves me forward.

And the women?

The women make me feel alive.

What about Hollywood, Fear?

It has nothing to do with me, Agostini. It was a joke. Don't you remember?

I never know when you are serious and when you are joking.

Neither do I.

What about the book?

What book?

Your book.

It's a love story, but I haven't finished it yet. Well, I might have finished it. I don't know.

A love story?

Yes. Don't tell anyone, Agostini. Promise.

I promise.

A man falls in love with a woman. The woman falls in love with the man. They are happy. Then they see that happiness is a gift they cannot share. They part. And they never see each other again.

Why can't they share their happiness?

Because they both want different things.

What does it matter what they want? Either they're in love or they're not in love.

It's not that simple.

Of course it is. You've got it wrong, Fear.

Maybe.

I just did some photographs of a model, naked. I hardly even noticed her, she made no impression on me. She was just a model. Then I saw her putting on her clothes and I realized it was the most sensual thing I had ever seen. She became embarrassed as I looked at her, and at that precise moment I understood her beauty.

Did she take off her clothes for you later?

No. She disappeared. And now I can't stop thinking about her standing there in my studio, putting on her clothes, her cheeks flushed with embarrassment. Do you think I'm ridiculous?

Of course.

I don't know where she went, but I see her photograph everywhere. She's on the side of every bus in Paris, advertising the Dupont supermarket chain.

Naked?

Naked.

Strange destiny for a woman. I hope you're not heartbroken, Agostini.

It's not such a bad thing to be heartbroken.

You have your photography. And you're good at it.

Writing is more interesting.

Why?

Because it is more personal and it lasts.

Photographs last. I like photographs. In fact, I would like to be a photographer. It seems to make more sense than all this scratching around trying to decide what love is. I mean, there's not a lot you can say about it. You're right. It's very simple. We only make it complicated because it is in our nature to do so.

You know what it's like, Fear. If you're honest with yourself. All you have to do is like you say: describe it.

I think I fell in love too, Agostini. But the trouble is, she's a fictional character.

What's the harm in that? That's what everyone does anyway. They turn a person into their own idea of a person. That's what I did with my model.

So, what are you up to? Why do I keep running into you in Rocket Street?

I'm going up to Père Lachaise to take some pictures.

Do the ghosts keep still for the camera?

There's a girl buried up there.

I'm sorry, Agostini.

I never knew her. She died young. It was an accident.

Death is always an accident.

Not always. There's a photograph of her in a frame, and I swear she's the most beautiful woman I ever saw.

More than the model putting her clothes on?

More than the model. I'm going to take a picture of her. Just for myself.

That's a good idea, Agostini.

Do you think so?

Yes. That way, if you fall in love with her, you won't get your heart broken.

You're right, Fear. You're not always right when it comes to love, but you know enough to see you through. Well, I'd better go.

See you around, Agostini.

See you around, Fear.

41 ✢

The Pigalle Girl stepped out of the apartment and walked away from Pigalle and the early morning. It became hot again, and she kept to the shade as she headed down toward the Opéra. She walked along the streets of Paris, and she felt sadness and freedom and the whole day spread in front of her as if it were the first of a new life.

Turning into avenue de l'Opéra, she headed down toward the rue de Rivoli, and she passed the travel agency near the bottom of the street with beaches and sand in the windows and smiling couples looking up from swimming pools. Then she crossed rue de Rivoli and walked through the courtyard of the Louvre, stopping at the glass pyramid in the center. She looked through the pyramid, up and into the sky, and she saw a plane in the distance flying away to the west.

She followed the plane until it vanished behind the line of buildings that stretched down the rue de Rivoli to the place de la Concorde. She would never know whether or not it was the pilot's plane but she decided to make it the pilot's plane so that she could finally say goodbye to him, whichever plane it was didn't matter, just so long as she got it over with and gave her heart the chance to follow it into the distance. And after it was gone, she still stood there looking up through the glass of the pyramid, saying good-

bye to the pilot even though she couldn't tell if it was the right one or not. Whether it is or it isn't, it still has a pilot in it, and all pilots are probably the same in the end, they wear the same uniform and they do the same things and take lovers in faraway places, even if they are not all fighter pilots who have seen death loom up in a cloud over the horizon and now spend their days searching the sky for the perfect martini.

The glass of the pyramid was clear as crystal, for it was only the day before that it had been cleaned, and she saw her reflection in it. She thought about the Louvre and the paintings that hung inside it, and she asked herself whether she should go inside and look at them. Then she tried to forget about the paintings and the pilot and the pyramid by turning away and continuing south to the river.

Fear was writing with one of the pencils Madame Jaffré had mailed to him and that he had found in his letter box the day before.

These are good pencils, Fear. They're the same brand as the ones Nabokov used to write *Lolita*. Perhaps you will find a nymphet to trip off your fingers with them. They can produce any letter you want, even an *r*.

The girl who was always smiling was standing beside him. She was plain, she would always be plain, but she was radiant and she was smiling as she looked at Fear, making him think that she knew all there was to know about him.

What will it be?

Pastis.

Finished with your coffee?

Finished.

Does coffee make a web?

It speeds up the web that is already being made by something else. It's for spiders on the move.

Are you on the move, Fear?

Don't know yet. Could be.

Someone was looking for you yesterday.

Who?

Didn't leave his name.

What did he look like?

He didn't look like a friend.

Must be Harm.

42 ❧

Agostini had his face pressed against the glass of the mausoleum and was peering inside at the photograph in a frame on the ground.

The photograph was of a young woman who had died in an accident in the 1920s, and this was explained in ink, purple with time past, in a spidery hand — words to the effect that she had been cruelly taken from her fiancé as she crossed a street.

She wore a dress of the period, and her hair was short and parted to one side. A long necklace fell to her chest. She was small and slender and fragile, and she looked out from where she lay in a frame in a tomb as if she were staring right into Agostini's eyes. The photograph was black and white and dulled with age, its corners dampened with the humidity, yet it exuded a beauty that took Agostini's breath away.

Che bona! he whispered.

The girl and the photograph and where it was set were everything that his world was not — modest, unassuming, private, tender — and he felt its power as he stood there, quite still, staring at it. He had taken his camera from his bag and was trying to focus on it. There wasn't enough light, and he couldn't use the flash because it would reflect on the glass and spoil the picture. The mausoleum was in disrepair, the window on the door was cracked, and the door itself was bent. A chain had been affixed to it against the lintel and fastened with a rusty padlock. Agostini turned around to check that no one was watching him and then he took a piece of wood he found lying on the ground and used it to force the chain. The door opened easily and he stepped inside. He took his camera in both hands once again, framed and focused the shot. And then he took the picture. He knelt down and took another so that the photograph filled the picture frame, and then he zoomed in and took another of the girl's face. He took more pictures and finished the roll, and then he put his camera back in the bag.

Inside the bag was his portable telephone, and after he had put his camera back into it, the telephone rang. It was Heinrich, his agent.

Agostini told him that he was busy and it wasn't the right time to talk, and Heinrich apologized for disturbing him. He didn't think he was working that day, and he was surprised. He joked with Agostini by saying that if he were on a job he would have to make sure he passed on a commission to him, and from the tone of his voice Agostini knew he wasn't joking. Then he asked Agostini for Fear's number. Agostini asked him why he wanted it, and Heinrich explained that a film producer wanted to contact him, so Agostini gave him the number and finished the conversation. Before putting the telephone away, he turned it off so that it wouldn't ring again.

Why am I talking to my agent in a tomb in Père Lachaise?

He got up from the ground and stared down at the photograph again. Then he blew a kiss to the girl who had died in the street before turning slowly back to the door.

43 ✻

Fear sat on the terrace of the café. He had watched Agostini walk up the hill to the cemetery, he had scribbled some notes, he had drunk his pastis, and he had felt the sun sink a little in the sky, the heat melting the sidewalk, the pastis filling his insides with a glow of goodness. He looked down at the novel on his table, and he knew that the end would come to him soon.

To say that anything might happen is to fool oneself, he decided. The anything is up future's sleeve, a magic act we can see through but can't actually do ourselves.

He drank up and paid and returned to his

room to find a string of messages on his answering machine. Harm said he had had enough of waiting, that he knew Fear was in Paris and that he would come soon for his money. Madame Jaffré hoped that he was writing, but she also wanted to know when he was going to remit his monthly overdraft installment. His landlord was concerned about the overdue rent. Salt wanted to see him, presumably to give him the $500 he owed him for the film synopsis. And Agostini said he had been stuck for an hour in a tomb at the cemetery before being freed by a passing tourist.

Fear was pleased about Salt, but he felt a shiver of panic at the thought of Harm, to whom he owed so much. He felt tired and disoriented after the events of the day and the telephone messages, so he poured himself another shot of pastis and drank it while he stood at the window deciding what to do.

Then he finished his drink and stepped out of the apartment again. It was early evening now and getting cooler. He turned right down Rocket Street, past the demolished houses and the *clochards* and the secondhand bookshop and the butcher's that stank of chicken on a spit and always made him nauseous in the morning, the bikers' bar with the fat man in dungarees who had once been a bouncer and the bookshop for new books and the baker's with the poodle on its last legs and the couscous restaurant and another restaurant and still another and finally the store where he always owed money.

And while he walked, he thought about himself and his world, and he knew that all he had was his writing, however good or bad it might be; he knew that it was the only thing that kept him going, aside from the money Agostini had given him, the four Lucky Lights in a pocket to his side and his heart, which beat somewhere behind his top pocket. He took out a cigarette and lit it with a match begged from a stranger, and he continued to walk westward, away from the places he had learned so well and from the bums demanding favors, and he didn't look back, he had nothing and he was nothing, and he felt curiously uplifted, the street comforted him in its hostile, overbearing loneliness, for what could be worse and what could be better than this? He knew that all he would ever need was a pastis and a cigarette and a piece of paper that hadn't already been written on. Whatever he had been before, whatever would become of him, was quite meaningless, all was dead and buried, the past was a book of reference collecting dust on a shelf, the present was a blank piece of paper waiting to be filled, and the future was a void. It didn't exist at all, and why should it, what was a Wednesday after a Tuesday when no one, not even the president of the republic, could be sure that tomorrow, like the newspaper, would land on the doorstep?

'Soir, Monsieur? Comment ça va?

Très bien. Très bien, said Fear, rushing off around the corner without waiting to discuss the matter.

He felt perfectly fine as he strode down the

boulevard with the money in his wallet and his notes and his pencil in his top pocket and his cigarettes in the other pocket and a warm feeling in his heart and a cool feeling in his stomach that came from the ice the girl with the smile had put in his pastis.

I'll go through some work on the other side of the river, and I'll think up some eroticism to add to my book, he thought. An erotic book consists of erotic passages interlarded with nonerotic passages, so that people have to search for the parts that will please them. If it is all erotic then it is no longer erotic, and just as Agostini's model becomes sensual as she puts on her clothes, I will dress my narrative and then undress it again when I feel the right moment for it. This is what I have to ensure. And I am better off considering that on the other side of the river; I am going to cross that bridge and get to the other side so that I can think more clearly, because the other side is the better side and the Right Bank has more ghosts in it. Something always good happens when I reach the Left Bank, there is always something waiting for me, whether or not I have gone to the trouble to arrange it.

He came to a café he knew, and he stopped for a pastis. Then he walked to another café. He read his notes and his last chapters, which he had brought with him, while drinking his pastis, and the reading and the drinking and the scribbling were combined into one fluid movement that made sense to him.

And then he continued along the boulevard Saint-Germain until he reached rue de Seine, where he turned right, down to the market bar. He took a terrace table and watched the people pass from one street to the next, and he felt as good as he could ever feel as the sun went down, sending its last, faltering rays past the edge of the round table in front of him and along the sidewalk in the shape of thin, protracted shadows. He looked up at all the people who passed, some holding hands, some with their heads in the sky, others looking down at their feet and their shopping. He looked down at his work. And then he looked at his glass and he called the waiter for another drink.

PART VI

44 ❧

Paris hardly changes. The same people come and go, in different guises, losing themselves under its protective, gray roof. I look out at it, and I see people arrive and leave, using it as a stage in their lives to look back on, a memory filled with the same images, a narrow street leading to an empty café, a bridge suspended over the darkened river, a boat appearing between its piers and spreading its wake from one bank to the other. A tourist stops to capture the city with a camera, and the city captures the tourist for a while, leading him by the hand and showing off its sights, a little jaded, so used it is to being pointed and stared at, yet nonetheless pleased at the thought of selling itself to those with enough cash. Henry Miller called it a whore. I call it a model, beautiful to look at yet secretly yearning to do something else with her time.

45 ❧

Upriver, eastward, Harm sat in the bar he owned, now closed down by the police. Harm was a Dutchman. He had lived many lives and now he lived in Paris. Fear had met him in London, many years earlier. He had offered his services as a character witness when Harm was accused of stealing a painting. And when they had gone to the pub afterward, Harm had told Fear that one day he would do him a favor in return. Harm had been acquitted because the painting turned out to be a forgery.

You'd be in jail now if you knew anything about art, Fear had told him.

Harm had been pleased to lend Fear some money a year earlier and had loaned him more money afterward. But when the police took away his license and closed down his bar, Harm realized he would need the money back so he could get out of Paris. So he called Fear and asked him for the money. And he called him again. And then he lost his patience with Fear, because he thought he was avoiding him. When Harm had first known him, Fear had had money, and Harm thought he must be hiding some now. And if Fear didn't have any money, he would just have to find it. That wasn't Harm's concern. He just wanted his back. That's all.

Harm didn't necessarily think of Fear as a friend. There wasn't room for that at the moment. Perhaps there never had been, and there certainly wasn't now. Besides, why should Harm have to hustle to earn a living while Fear just sat in his apartment writing poetry? No one should write poetry when they owed other people money, especially a friend, even if they weren't really friends any longer.

So Harm sat in his bar thinking of how he could get the money back from Fear and how he could escape from Paris without paying the fine that had been imposed on him by the police.

On the table in front of him was a piece of paper with figures on it, constituting all the money Fear owed him. The first loan was for 12,500 francs, which Fear said he needed to pay back all those from whom he had borrowed during the preceding year. The second loan, made almost immediately after the first, was for 10,000 francs, and the final loan, corresponding to the best days of the bar when Harm had made the most money, was for 30,000 francs, making a total of 52,500 francs.

He might have helped me out once, thought Harm. And I paid him back. Now he owes me something.

46 ❧

Fear listened to the rain falling on the skylight and down to the cobbles below and he thought of many things, of the sublime and the ridiculous, as he lay there upon the bed.

He looked up at the ceiling and then glanced over to the thin curtain that was just an old sheet hanging from two hooks above the window, so that the light of the couryard shone through it like the sun, casting an ethereal glow within the room. A car passed now and then down the street, but the rain drowned it out before it reached the next block. And the rain still fell, louder and louder, dripping through the walls of the building into a saucepan he had placed by the bed, like the last bullets of a war being counted out in a helmet.

The bottle of pastis was empty and there were two glasses, one standing half full, one fallen, broken, beside it. Clothes lay strewn about the room, a pair of clogs discarded in haste, a skirt hanging limply over a chair and, next to the bottle of pastis, a garter belt, along with Fear's shirt, its buttons scattered on the uneven tiled floor. Elsewhere were pages of manuscript, some of which had fallen from the table to the floor and others that had been carried over to the bed.

She tore all my buttons off, he said to himself. Every single one.

He was immobile and there was nothing much he could do about it. She had tied his wrists together with one of her silk stockings and attached them to the head of the old iron bedstead, and his ankles were attached to the other end. Without the whiskey and the pastis, he would doubtless have felt considerable pain, for she had ensured he was securely fastened. He had been effectively racked, and his demands to be released had been met with nothing more than a smile.

She sat on the bed, bending down to take a mouthful of pastis and drop her cigarette into the ashtray. Fear stared at her breasts and the curvature of her back and at the perfectly sculpted nape of her neck as her long, dark hair fell forward, hiding her face. Then she turned to him.

She drew circles with her finger over his chest and moved it downward to tease him.

She had picked up a page of manuscript from

the floor and was reading from it and, as she did so, she began to play with him, drawing circles with her index finger across his torso. He felt the sharpness of her long fingernail painted the color of blood, and as her finger moved along his body past his hips to his thighs and back again, his body ached and agonized with the waiting. When she lowered her mouth to his chest, it was her tongue that now traced patterns over his skin. His prick was impossibly hard as her tongue reached its tip, and he thought he would come as soon as she took it in her mouth, but he somehow suppressed the orgasm, sending it back to where it belonged, to return when he knew nothing on earth could control it.

Relax, Fear, she whispered, drawing away from him. Relax.

She took the cigarette from the ashtray and bent forward to place it between his lips.

What about a drink? he asked, as she took the cigarette from him and let it fall into the empty glass.

All gone, she replied.

She now positioned herself on all fours above him, the page of manuscript held tightly in her right hand. His tongue reached for her nipple and caught it for a second, and their lips met in a perfunctory kiss as she slipped back down his body. She teased him with her tongue as his prick strained to meet it, and then she sat astride him. She slid with aching slowness onto his prick and he gasped as she sat fully upon it, moving gently up and down so that the tip appeared on the lips of her vulva, glistening with her moisture and purple with an expectancy and desire that made him breathless.

She was holding the page of manuscript and looking up at the ceiling. Then she withdrew from him and looked into his eyes with a smile, glancing at the page and reading from it.

He tried to draw her to him, to kiss her, but she remained seated on top of him, looking to the walls and up to the ceiling, the aching in his body turning him from side to side.

She moved forward to kiss his chest and then, very slowly, she slid back onto him. The page of manuscript was now creased in her fist and, as she moved back and forth, she cupped his balls with her other hand, with her fingernail stroking his prick as it appeared from her vulva. She put the page of manuscript in her mouth and chewed it, and Fear looked up at her, his eyes wide, his entire body straining to control the rush of his orgasm.

The rain came faster and the bullets fell into the helmet and onto the cobbles of the courtyard and the light that came through the sheet created a shadow against the wall, the shadow of her body as it moved upon him, raising herself to the end of his prick and holding it there so that it could be seen beneath her, a shaft of darkness angled on the wall. And as he looked at the two of them and the image they made, she began to move more quickly, one hand on his stomach, the other behind her. The page of manuscript fell from her mouth and she cried out, and as her fingernails dug into his skin, the pain arrested him for one, empty moment, so that it was only after she came again, in a second, lingering wave, that he was able, finally, to come inside her.

She waited for a while, her head raised to the ceiling, and then, quite abruptly, she withdrew from him. She got up from the bed and stood there, looking down at him. The pleasure ebbed through his body, and as it passed, he felt the advance of pain in his wrists and ankles, as poignant and as profound as the orgasm that had so recently consumed him.

Well? Are you going to untie me now?

She lit another cigarette, and Fear stared up at her as she blew a ring of smoke up toward the ceiling and turned back to face him. Her naked body was framed in the glow from the courtyard, the arc of her back, the side of one breast caught in shadow, and Fear marveled at her presence, for she now seemed like a perfect stranger to him, detached, distant, elusive.

She turned back to him and her smile turned into the faintest chuckle echoing around the walls of the studio as she bent down to pick up another page of manuscript. Then she sat upon the bed and, after reading the first lines on the page, glanced at him casually.

Later, Fear. Later. After all, what's the hurry?

47 ✣

The rain had stopped and Fear awoke, stirred by the emptiness and the stillness in the apartment. She was gone, and the lingering odor of her body that hung over the bed and the pillow seemed the only sign that she had ever been with him.

For once, at least, a dream and a moment of real time have become truly indistinguishable, he thought.

He lay there, looking at the patches of damp that spread across the walls and the ceiling, the stigmata of passing seasons and the presage of another autumn when they would grow still larger. And he imagined the water seeping further and further around the room until the whole place disintegrated, like a ship breaking up on a distant shore.

He got up and sat upon the bed for a while, rubbing his head and looking around the room, saw the empty bottle of pastis, the two glasses, and the ashtray filled with cigarette ends marked with bright red lipstick, and only then did he know he hadn't been dreaming. He bent down to pick up the pages of his manuscript that lay scattered about his feet and put them in order. When he saw that a page was missing, he searched the floor and the bed for it nervously. It was crumpled and torn and had lipstick on it, so he flattened it out before placing it carefully among the others. He saw a button on the floor, and he picked it up and shook his head before letting it fall to his feet. Then he got up and went over to the window, peering around the curtain into the courtyard. No one stirred outside, and he felt as alone in the world as it was possible to be. The sky was thin and white, neither cloudy nor clear, just the neutral tone of a summer dawn after the rain has come and gone and the sun has risen over the horizon.

He put on the shorts that did not belong to him and fastened them with his old tie. Then he carried his manuscript over to the table and sat in his chair and lit a cigarette. He put a fresh piece of paper into the typewriter and turned down the roller six double spaces.

The Pigalle Girl stood on the Pont des Arts facing west and looked up into the sky as dusk fell. She saw the trace of a huge vapor trail drawn in a line upward, above her head, and, as she followed it, she saw another cross it neatly, like a kiss on a postcard. She remembered standing on the bridge with the pilot and the pilot asking a stranger to take their picture, and she saw them together, the pilot holding her and smiling and calling out to the stranger, explaining how his camera worked, the echo of his voice still rising from the bridge into the clear summer air.

It's idiot-proof, he shouted. But you still have to hold it steady.

Then she turned away and walked to the Left Bank, onto the rue de Seine and up to the rue de Buci. She stopped at a café and drank a kir, and then she drank another, more quickly this time, feeling a stab in her heart. She dropped some coins onto the table from the money the pilot had left for her and moved on to another café, sitting in a corner and staring through the window. She drank another kir, and she sat before the empty glass, and time passed unnoticed by her. Eventually, a man asked her for a light.

Take it. But don't talk to me.

The man took the lighter and thanked her, and she paid up and left, without looking back. She walked past the hotel where she had made love with the pilot, and she thought of the seamless wallpaper and the garden that was a labyrinth in which two people could lose themselves.

That's love, she thought. Getting lost together.

She walked down the boulevard and headed back to the river. The sky was the deepest blue, and it hung over Paris in all its infinity, lit for passing moments by the bateaux mouches *that slid, one by one, under the bridge, silent tourists peering upward and, after them, a party of revelers dancing disjointedly to music that echoed from one quai to the other. She carried on, an unexpected surge of gaiety in her step as she recalled a moment from adolescence, a kiss stolen behind a wall somewhere, and made her way up the boulevard Sebastopol to the American bar.*

Make me a martini. Just as you did for the captain, she said to her friend who worked behind the bar.

She drank the martini and then she ordered another one, and a man with an accent started talking to her. She hadn't eaten all day, and she felt the ice-cold gin seep through her body as she looked into his eyes.

Our emotions are given a burial at sea, he was saying. With a barrel of gin and a nice cup of tea.

Qui êtes-vous? she heard herself asking, unable to speak a word of English.

A stranger in a bar trying to take advantage

of a girl who's probably thinking of a man she loves, or loved.

Américain?

English. Americans don't drink tea.

The man bought her a martini, and when she had finished it, he danced with her to a tune someone played on the jukebox. The lights of the bar turned in circles, and she fell into his arms. And then he led her outside and kissed her. His lips felt strange and foreign to her, and the revenge and the guilt she felt as she responded played tricks with her so that she couldn't tell whether she wanted him or was pretending to want him.

He led her by the hand to a hotel around the corner, and they kissed and tore at each other's clothes in a room near the top. She lay before him as if she were a gift, and he turned her over and entered her from behind, and she rose onto her knees with her head in the pillow as he grasped her hips and pulled her back and forth onto his prick. She felt the remorse overwhelm her, she didn't want to come, but as he came inside her, she felt herself slipping, away from the pain that seared her heart, crying out and clutching the sheet with her hands.

The Englishman fell asleep and the Pigalle Girl got up and walked over to the window. Dawn was breaking, and she looked down at the street cleaners hosing the pavements. She put on her clothes and slipped out of the room and walked through the place des Victoires, on and up to Pigalle, and as she headed homeward, the distraction of Paris awakening evaporated behind her, and all that was good and all that was bad about the night was lost, gone forever, swept up and washed down the street to the gutter. She climbed the stairs to her apartment, and her heart started sinking at the thought of being alone once again in her room. She opened the cupboard that hung by her door but the key wasn't hidden in the crack in the wall. She faltered for a moment, seized with panic. The front door was ajar.

He was sitting on the bed, smoking a cigarette, a smile spreading across his face. I can't go on a mission without my shaker. And besides, the plane had an engine problem.

The Pigalle Girl stood quite still, holding the door open behind her. And the pilot got up from the bed and took her in his arms, closing the door with a kick.

Why are you crying, girl? It doesn't matter. We can be together again. For a day or forever or for never if you want.

But I thought you'd gone.

So did I.

I looked at your plane through the pyramid and I thought it was you. I saw it vanish as it went behind the buildings. My heart went with it. It's gone now and I'll never get it back.

Your heart is still with you. It wasn't the right plane.

48 ✣

Fear typed the date on the bottom of the last page, just below the reunion of the Pigalle Girl and the pilot, and the final slamming of her apartment door. Then he typed a title page. He decided to create a title that didn't have an *r* in it, because it would look strange if he used an asterisk and he didn't want to write it by hand. He couldn't do anything about his name, but he had already decided to use a pseudonym.

He thought about the kind of name he could use, and he considered the advantages of using a woman's nom de plume, because readers might be more interested in an erotic novel written by a woman. Then he realized it wouldn't work, because books invariably have photographs of the author on the dust jacket. He could always get Agostini to give him a picture of someone, perhaps the woman he had gone to photograph in the cemetery, but after careful thought he decided against complicating matters.

He wanted to put "an erotic novel" on the cover, and he thought an asterisk in this context might actually be appropriate. He knew that there were many novels published that had erotic passages in them that weren't necessarily classified as erotic novels, but his novel was clearly erotic and there was no point in shying away from the fact. His bank manager had suggested he write an erotic novel and that is what he had done, and he was going to deliver it to her as such and get his checkbook back.

NIGHT IN PIGALLE

An E*otic Novel

By

Mason Line

Mason Line sounded so unlikely that it seemed perfectly convincing to him, and he was pleased with the way that it looked on the page.

He had a copy of the manuscript, because he had used carbon paper, so he took the copy and tied it up neatly with a piece of string. He stubbed out his cigarette and took a shower, washing his hair with the last piece of soap, which broke in his hand and disappeared down the plug hole. He stood there trembling under the ice-cold water and rubbed his body with his hands to make himself clean. Then he dried himself quickly and took out his old linen suit and dressed, taking the tie from the shorts that did not belong to him and slipping it around his collar. He found a handkerchief in a drawer and folded it into his top pocket, and he brushed his hair, glancing in the mirror to check his appearance. He remembered what his father had told him to say when shaving in front of a mirror.

Where do I come in?

Then he wiped his brogues with a rag, picked

up his manuscript, put it in a plastic bag, and stepped out of his building into Rocket Street.

Salt was waiting for him in the café. They took a table in the back, which was divided into booths, and Salt explained all that had to be explained to get Fear to sign the contract.

You said you wanted cash, said Salt. If you would sign here, on both copies.

Fear took the pen Salt offered him and read the contract while Salt sat impatiently opposite him.

It's a standard contract, Fear.

There's no such thing, replied Fear.

When he had read through the contract, he signed it where indicated and he gave Salt one copy and kept the other for himself. Then Salt gave him a manila envelope with the money in it.

You can count it if you like. It's all there. The $500 I owe you for the treatment plus $10,000 that I am giving you, not on the first day of principal photography but now, as an act of good faith. That makes 10,500, which converted to francs is 52,500.

Good faith? You're paying me off, Salt. That's not good faith. That's good business.

Salt smiled and Fear counted the money. Yes, it's all there. Thanks.

Well, thanks to you for a truly great idea. I mean, a girl from the nineties falling in love with a film star from the silent era. Perfect.

Buster Keaton was not just a film star, Salt.

Absolutely. But we might have to make a few changes. We're not sure about the jealous boyfriend following the girl through the cinema 161 screen and being chased out of Hollywood by the Keystone Cops. Or Buster Keaton's wife getting lost in Paris. We'll keep "The Dream Divine" as a working title. But we're keeping the Buster Keaton imitator as the stand-in projectionist.

What about the script?

They'll need someone with a name.

I have a name.

Of course you do. But you know how it works.

Yes, I know. Someone pertinent perhaps?

Salt got up from the table. He proffered his hand and Fear shook it without standing up. Then he was gone.

I am now 52,500 francs and one erotic novel better off than I was an hour ago, he thought, sipping his pastis and looking out through the doorway of the café as Salt disappeared into Rocket Street. He still had the manila envelope open in one hand under the table and the cash in the other, and he stared at the money for a long while before slipping the cash back into the envelope.

Hello, Fear? What's up?

It was Harm.

I thought you'd be here, he said. If you weren't in your apartment.

Hello, Harm.

Harm sat down next to Fear. He had seen the money.

Yes, I should have called you, Harm. But you know how it is.

Yes.

It's 52,000, isn't it?

Fifty-two thousand five hundred.

It's all there. You can count it if you like.

49 ⚶

Fear knew that was how things worked. There was nothing you could do about it. To try to counter it was to interfere with nature, and when you interfered with nature, your life was not worth the paper it was printed on. So he simply got up from the table after giving Harm his money and walked out of the café.

It was as hot as ever as he walked down Rocket Street. He stopped for a moment and took out the handkerchief he had put in his pocket and dabbed the perspiration from his temple. Something had fallen out with the handkerchief, and he bent down to see what it was. It was the lottery ticket. He was in exactly the same spot he had been in when he had discovered it earlier. And there it was, once again, lying in the gutter. It had never been his at all, and now it was back where it belonged, a losing number cast aside by a stranger.

He walked to the river and stood on the bridge, looking up at the sky and thinking about the pilot. He had never met a pilot, but he had become friends with a Vietnam veteran when he had lived in New York ten years earlier. The veteran had had a way of looking right through him; what he had seen in war clouded everything he said and everything he did. He had a good sense of humor but a permanent sadness to his expression, even when he smiled. He had told Fear that he could never love again, and Fear had believed him. When he created the pilot, Fear remembered the veteran and decided to make of him a man who was no longer capable of losing himself in love. And this is what the Pigalle Girl came to understand.

He had wanted the pilot to return to the apartment, he had brought them back together, but it was clear the pilot would leave again and never return. He would pick up his cocktail shaker, put on his hat, and walk out of the apartment, and the Pigalle Girl would stay where she was, away from the window, so she wouldn't have to follow him as he got into the taxi.

He walked on over the bridge and up to the rue des Ecoles, thinking about Salt and the idea he had sold to him. He had stopped by the cinema and was looking up at a poster for a new film and he remembered once again how he had walked the streets of Paris wondering about what Salt had said to him.

I like to give people what they want.

It was only logical that people wanted what they couldn't have. They wanted to see a certain amount of money being spent, love being made, blood being spilled. They wanted to be voyeurs on a world that had the same rules as theirs but was inhabited by imaginary people, people of courage and flamboyance who didn't care what others thought of them. They wanted a peephole into another world that was brutal and solitary and elusive, filled with heroes and heroines who spoke in loud voices, filling the screen with desire and ambition, archetypes who had escaped the banality of everyday life and launched themselves into the illusion of moving pictures. These were the icons of a certain age, transient, ephemeral creatures who never had to worry about bank managers and landlords, who never displayed uncertainty, whose real lives, as reported in the interviews they gave, seemed even more fictional than the lives they assumed in order to be sufficiently "pertinent."

He moved away from the cinema and continued toward Saint-Germain. It was midday and there was no shade for him to walk in. He kept on walking, the bag holding his manuscript gripped tightly in one hand, a cigarette in the other, and when he entered the bank, Madame Jaffré was at her desk, looking into her computer, exactly as he had imagined her.

50 ❧

The tsunami is a wave that results from earthquakes on the seabed, occasioned by the shifting of the tectonic plates. It can be as high as a building and travel as fast as an airplane. On April 1, 1946, a tsunami more than fifteen meters high traveled 3,600 kilometers in four hours and thirty-four minutes, at an average speed of 784 kilometers an hour.

I found this information while reading the newspaper last night. I'm not sure one should necessarily believe all one reads in newspapers, and I find the data rather overwhelming, but I like the thought of the tsunami racing across the ocean.

I imagined being carried on the crest of a tsunami from Washington State, where I was born, to Akashi Bay, riding its white crest and shielding my brow from the sun as I sped across the Pacific. I remembered, as a little girl, standing on the beach and looking out to where the sun dipped below the horizon and asking my parents where it went, and this, curiously enough, this is how I see my death, whenever it comes to take me away with it, a journey over the edge of the world to a place of infinite peace and untold pleasures.

I lay in my apartment, thinking half aloud, talking, not necessarily to myself but to my other half, to that invisible interlocutor with whom I have shared so many lives, that person who could be me, or the shadow of me. For what constitutes existence if it is not a lopsided conversation between oneself and ones reflection? In my bed, so late at night, I could hear nothing but the absence of sound and, beyond it, or within it, a still, small voice that was but a hum, the proof that I was alive, that some hidden organism was begging questions of me.

Sometimes, I feel that my imagination is flagging, like a muscle that has been pulled by the rigors of my waking, working life, yet the present often rescues me, I find I can still lose myself within its fickle embrace. It is a tense that, however lean and unforgiving, still offers me simple joys — a vodka and tonic, a page from a book, a walk at twilight, a glimpse of the sun falling neatly between two shuttered buildings, a thought stilled by a face smiling at me from the hidden depths of a computer screen.

I was born and raised in the Pacific Northwest and I moved away, or ran away, or ran toward San Francisco, in the mid-1970s. I waited on tables, made a killing in tips, took LSD, and fell in love with Paris in the shape of a diminutive Frenchman with a charming smile and an absurd accent, called Hubert Jaffré.

Hubert Hubert wanted to be Yves Klein, he was an artist of limitless intelligence and limited talent, and he waded through the imponderables of existence forever afraid of drowning, even though the water rarely came up above his knees. Life to him was an enigma that he tried to solve through the abstraction of art, yet his art was clearly too abstract, and whereas at least the mythical Yves employed blue, Hapless Hubert went for black as if, within its uncompromising dullness, he would find an opposing enlightenment, for he believed strongly in the principle of opposites, if not much else.

I am being unkind. But I am a different person now from the starry-eyed tyro who was once impressed with practically everything and who saw in a Frenchman's eyes a legendary romance that would whisk her away to Paris and to the world inhabited by Hemingway, Miller, and Zelda Fitzgerald, even though the first and the last had long since been transported to Akashi Bay by the time I entered the scene. Zelda was always a favorite and still is, because in her writing I see the perfectly timed observations of a woman teetering between clarity and madness. I must have read one or two stories aloud to my feckless Frenchman in the hope of teasing him into a more humorous view of life, but where Zelda succeeded, I failed.

Hubert Hubert and I soon entered into what is called a marriage of convenience, an unfortunate collision of ideas that resulted in a green card for Hubert, who quite preemptorily (but not inconveniently) decided that the New World was too, well, new for him. What was fortuitous was that, while he was granted permission to *install himself*, as he so quaintly put it, in the home of the brave, I earned (earned is appropriate in this context) the inalienable right to do the same thing in France.

I came to Paris, following Hubert in his slippery wake, out of spite, boredom, and that Calvinist sense of meanness that demands the exaction of opportunity, all this quite apart from the fact that Zelda and the gang beckoned. Handy Hubert received me with open arms, and we lived in perfect misery together for two years, long enough for me to learn the ropes, as it were. High-rolling Hubert's uncle got me a job at a bank, of all things, so that by the time Cupid was asking for his deposit back, I was in a position to go it alone. As for Humble Hubert, he continued to produce paintings that apparently no one understood, suffering greatly but not enough to produce anything interesting. I still see him occasionally. The last time we met, we talked of those summer evenings in Union Square in 1978, of the love that had once bound us, and of that blissful naïveté that made life stop in its tracks and art seem the promise of all things. I often wonder whether he will wake up one morning to discover that he really is Yves Klein. And, when that happens, the *vide* is going to hit him like a Mack truck.

51 ✂

I took the job at the bank as I would have taken a job as a waitress or anything else, for that matter; it was just a means of earning money. I thought it might last a year or so, but I found time pass at a speed I could never have imagined. Once my French was fluent, I found that my innate knack for figures and a memory hardly dulled by the excesses of my youth meant that I became oddly indispensable. I say oddly, because if anyone had told me that this is what I would end up doing, I would have told them they had a clearer idea of the absurd than even poor Zelda. In short, they promoted me, putting me in a position of responsibility, handling clients and overseeing their accounts.

My predecessor at this branch on the Left Bank, Antonio Pires, was moved sideways, and I stepped into his seat in the spring, moving from another branch across the river. Fear was one of the first clients I encountered. When he told me he was a writer, I suggested he write something commercial to solve his financial problems. To my astonishment, he did.

I came to know him quite well, much better

than I have intimated in this narrative. We spent the evening together following our drink at the Armistice. We talked of many things, and he told me about his life, about his work and his loves, about Salt and Harm and Gisèle and his friend Agostini and many other things, opening up his heart to me as the evening progressed. He said that he never talked about his work to anyone and he wondered why he did so to me. I was touched, of course. I liked him, I liked his honesty and his ability to explain himself, as if he were defending his life, as if he had been attacked in some way for being who he was.

I told him about the book of haiku, and when I mentioned Akashi Bay, he said it was the principal theme in the book he was writing. Naturally I thought it an extraordinary coincidence, but he corrected me.

Senhor Pires gave me a compact disc of fado music, he told me. I have no interest in fado music and I have no compact disc player, for that matter, yet I wanted to give him something in return that was precious to me. So I gave him the book of haiku, most of which I know by heart, anyway.

I was the first to read Fear's erotic novel and honored when I saw he had dedicated it to me. I enjoyed it for its weaknesses as well as its strengths, and for all that I learned of the man who had written it. He must have been infatuated with the Pigalle Girl. Why else would he have fantasized so much about her being with someone else?

The book was a success, or at least successful

enough for him to leave Paris for a while. He came back to the bank a month ago to pay off his overdraft and take me out to lunch.

You were kind to me, Amor. You understand more than most.

I remember every detail of that night we spent together. Perhaps I was coy not to describe it more fully. Was it inevitable that we should return to his room after dinner? Probably. He was anxious for me to read passages from his book, although whether he actually wanted me to tie him up is another matter. To be perfectly frank, Fear was not a remarkable lover. He lacked imagination. Yet he was certainly agreeable, or at least as agreeable as a writer can be when he is stealing secrets from you. But then, isn't that what a banker does, when she isn't stealing your money?